PRAISE ᵢ ᵤ ₖ ₖₑₙₑₑ BERNARD

Raves for the Jaded Gentleman Novels

Obsession Wears Opals
"Passion and adventure seamlessly blend as Bernard stirs a tale steeped in intrigue and secrets, keeping pages turning and interest high." –*RT BookReviews*

"Renee Bernard has redefined what makes a hero and heroine heroic..." –*Tina Ong, GoodReads*

Passion Wears Pearls
"Chemistry between the characters sparks and crackles with a vibrant energy that shivers up your spine keeping you on the edge of your seat well into the night." –*Veiled Secret Reviews*

"Renee Bernard hits another one out of the park!" –*Lindsey Ross, GoodReads*

Ecstasy Wears Emeralds
"Sensuality fills the pages." –*Publishers Weekly*

"Level of emotional force that makes sure you cannot put this book down!...Ms. Bernard skillfully weaves a tale of love and learning, friendship and betrayal to lead you down a merry path..."

Seduction Wears Sapphires

"An amazing read, I enjoyed it immensely...Ashe and Caroline are wonderful characters that made me fall in love with them from the beginning of the story." –*Night Owl Reviews*

"A fine book, well crafted, well researched, and an entertaining romantic novel...Historical romance fans will be delighted, I have no doubt." –*The Book Binge*

"What a refreshing new take on two people who from first sight are determined to detest each other...I was immediately engrossed with the fiery, witty dialogue and the curiosity of how this couple, who loathed each other upon their meeting, would come full circle to a beautifully shared love in the end." –*Ficion Vixen*

Revenge Wears Rubies

"Sensuality fairly steams from Bernard's writing. This luscious tale will enthrall you. Enjoy!" –Sabrina Jeffries, *New York Times* bestselling author

"If you're a fan of spicy hot romances mixed with a bit of intrigue and set in Victorian London, don't miss this one!" –*The Romance Dish*

"Galen's journey from emotional cripple to ability to love is captivating, erotic romance." –*Fresh Fiction*

LADY FALLS

BOOK ONE IN THE BLACK ROSE TRILOGY

RENEE BERNARD

This book is dedicated to my dear friend and twin sister, Lisa Watson. I know what you're going to say. The twin thing is a little bit of wishful thinking on my part but I'm not letting it go. Because it took less than three minutes for me to figure out that we've been friends forever—or we should lie and make that claim. It's a connection I don't need logic to explain. The heart knows what the heart knows. So here's what I know: No one will cheer louder or longer for you, no one will make you laugh harder and no one will convince me that your friendship means I haven't made something of myself in this world.

Villains are not born—they are made. And in the case of a Villainess, she is crafted and carved out of the fires of a broken heart and God help the man who thinks to trespass, bruise her further and then survive the encounter.

Most villains swing with a club in blind rage and think to overwhelm you with brute force. But a true Villainess can cut you with a blade so fine that it will be some time before you realize that you are already dead.

And you will remember the kiss of that weapon with fondness...and long for her return.

— PHILLIP WARRICK

PROLOGUE

1859
Manchester, England

"You ungrateful baggage!"

Raven bit the inside of her lip as the Head Mistress's words echoed in her head. *Stupid woman. Baggage is a thing. Things can't be grateful—or ungrateful, really. And if they were I'm betting her corset would be grateful for mercy after trying to hold in that fat belly of hers all day...*

"What are you smirking about, you slip of trash!?"

Mrs. Hoggerty had a thousand insults she spewed on the useless vile little human-animals in her tender Christian care. The orphans who had been blessed to be dropped off at the Greenwood Charity House were regularly exposed to the Head Mistress's opinions on the worth of illegitimate children and their immoral natures—and as a result, Raven was nearly immune to most of them.

"I was...trying not to cry," Raven said, forcing her eyes to look at the edge of her shoes. It was a weak performance and she knew it, but a bout of poorly timed giggles could end with broken ribs if she weren't careful. "I'm very sorry, Mrs. Hoggerty."

"You will be, Raven Wells! You will be sorry! I'll see to that if I see to nothing else!" Mrs. Hoggerty grabbed her by her thin upper arm and began to haul the ten year old from the dormitory.

Raven risked a quick glance over her shoulder to try to reassure her friends that she was taking the turn in her fortunes in stride—and not to cry.

Don't cry, Pepper. See? I'm not scared of her and it was worth it to have a little fun! Pepper was only five and she'd cry herself sick if she could.

Mrs. Hoggerty had caught Raven teaching the others to dance. It had been a fun game to pretend they were at a country dance and prance about in between their beds, using a flannel sheet like a cape and making faces at the little ones to make them laugh.

Well, fun until...

"It's whores that dance, Raven Wells! It's in your blood, I suppose, but that you would cavort about like that in front of the others and—and encourage them to do the same!" Mrs. Hoggerty's pace was so quick that Raven had to struggle just to stay on her feet sure that if she fell Mrs. Hoggerty would break her arm just for spite.

"L-ladies dance, don't they?"

"Hah!" Mrs. Hoggerty snorted. "You ain't no lady! Nice old parson and his wife took you in as a baby and filled your head with an education fit for nothing but parlors and tea parties but it's all shit! Died suddenly without leaving a farthing or a word, didn't they? Nothing for the little bastard they thought to turn into a fine little lady? Well, you'll see you're no better than the rest of 'em and you'll mind them sly looks you keep sending me!"

"I'm s-sorry, Mrs. Hoggerty," she offered, the hitch in her voice from nearly stumbling as they passed through the open door into the outer courtyard of the house.

"Two years you've been here and don't think I ain't wise to you, you little slut!"

Eyes down, Raven's brow furrowed. She wasn't sure why at ten years of age a person could qualify as a "slut" or how to redeem the sins of parents she'd never known. Her blood was fouled according to

Mrs. Hoggerty but the Reverend Porter and his wife had said only the sweetest things to her and called her their little angel. It was hard to know whom to believe.

But whatever kindness and care she'd grown up with was nearly forgotten now. Mrs. Hoggerty and Greenwood believed that the only things that might save her soul from the black stain of her birth were hard work, hunger and prayer.

Raven Wells was young but she'd already decided she liked none of those things.

The bell rang to summon the children to morning prayers and a breakfast of weak porridge and crusts but Raven knew better than to ask.

The morning was cold and the gray skies threatened rain as Mrs. Hoggerty pulled her up onto the single square flagstone that was raised a few inches at the small muddy yard's center. It wasn't much of a pedestal but it served Mrs. Hoggerty's purposes.

"You'll stand here until I come for you." Mrs. Hoggerty's grip on her arm was released at last and Raven almost cried out at the pain of her blood rushing back that made her fingers feel like they were on fire. "Don't you dare move! I find you off this block and I'll get the flogging stick and beat you until you're down for good, you hear me?"

Raven nodded. "Yes, Mrs. Hoggerty."

"Not. One. Toe. Off." Mrs. Hoggerty punctuated each word with a poke of her thick finger against Raven's chest.

Raven nodded again, not answering this time.

She's hoping I'll get cheeky and give her an excuse for it.

Mrs. Hoggerty finally left her alone, the fat woman's boot steps echoing off of the gray stone walls of the yard. Windows reflected the gray clouds and added to the otherworldly effect of her cube-shaped world.

Time passed and she had trouble tracking it without a sun in the sky.

Raven sighed and it began to rain.

As punishments went, this one was of her favorites.

She didn't mind the rain.

Raven tipped her face up to the skies and imagined the rain was washing away weeks of Greenwood grime and sweat from her features. She used the tips of her fingers to scrub her cheeks and wash behind her ears, undoing her braids to make the most of the bath. She stroked the back of her neck and stretched her hands upward, a pagan goddess taking each drop as her due and laughing at the downpour.

LORD TRENT'S breath caught in his throat.

The overstuffed wraith at his side was practically panting in fury. "I'll beat her for it! Do you see her, sir? Do you see what a shameless animal she is?" Mrs. Hoggerty crossed her arms. "She's a witch!"

He nodded with a smile, his eyes never leaving the little figure perched on her stone reveling in the storm. Her impromptu dance was almost gypsy-like and he was immediately taken with her. "Calm yourself, madam. She is…free-spirited."

He'd hoped she'd have a bit of her father's bearing and braced himself for disappointment but this—this was a gift from the gods. She had aristocratic lines and even at the gangly age of ten, he could see beyond the raw coltish beauty to her potential.

My god, the glorious potential!

She was almost feral in her pleasure, an unashamed vixen cavorting in the cold spring rain as unaware of her beauty and appeal as a cub of its claws.

She'll suit my plans perfectly.

Lord Trent shook his head. He'd nearly missed it. When a friend had confessed of his bastard daughter's existence and begged him to look into the fate of a child he'd lost track of after some vague tragedy, he'd promised to see to the girl—without a single thought of wasting a moment on it.

But a few weeks later and a dark turn of events, the Earl of Trent had begun to think about revenge and what the perfect game would look like. And he'd remembered his promise and the existence of a girl without legitimate family. And his imagination had seized on the notion of using her like a bit player in a grander scheme...

It would take time, true cunning, craft, and best of all, just the right pieces on the board. The wait would be long but it would make the taste of vengeance all the sweeter.

He'd always been obsessed with games but in the pitch black of an empty ball room, the Earl of Trent had decided that he was just the man to demonstrate to the world what dark justice could look like when mastered by a genius in a gentleman's form. The world preached forgiveness but Geoffrey couldn't remember the taste of it. In recent years, he'd begun to accept only the dictates of his own needs and the inner voices that ruled him.

And ever since he'd met Phillip Warrick...

A passing dislike had coalesced into pure hatred for the young rake and Trent gave in to the intricate and convoluted scenario that unfolded in his mind with a seductive allure that soothed the storm in his head. He would build a labyrinth of pain that he would guide Phillip Warrick into and deprive him of his happiness.

I'll teach him what humiliation truly is...

Trent's gaze narrowed as he leaned closer to the glass window, and his smile widened. He would need a few years to polish and train her for what he had in mind, but who's to say he couldn't enjoy it?

Mrs. Hoggerty saw his smile and matched it with a wicked knowing look of her own. "Free spirited? She suits you, does she? Looking for a scullery maid, your lordship?"

"Please gather what things she has and prepare her to leave, Mrs. Hoggerty."

"Hah! She's got nothing and I ain't just handing her over without—"

He unfolded his wallet and took out a few notes. Her immediate silence was almost comical.

Almost.

She'd sell me a dozen girls without blinking even if I told her I was procuring them for a blood sacrifice.

"Prepare her to leave." He shed any pretext of civility, deciding it was a waste. "Now."

Her mouth dropped open making her look like a bovine fish gaping for air but she dropped a quick curtsey as her face flushed red. "As you wish, your lordship. I'll get her then."

He shook his head. "I've changed my mind, Mrs. Hoggerty."

"Y-you don't want her?"

"Very much. But I think I'll fetch her myself." He straightened his coat to refasten it against the weather. "Our business is concluded. See to it my coachman is ready and the gates are open."

He breezed past her without another word, heading down a narrow stairwell toward the ground floor and the stony courtyard. He put on his hat and stepped into the rain.

"Tell me your name," he commanded, wondering if she'd yelp from surprise at his sudden appearance or turn into a mouse.

She lowered her arms slowly, finishing a careful pirouette before tilting her head like a small bird. Curiosity flashed in eyes the color of smoke. "It is Raven Wells. And your name?"

"I am Geoffrey Parke, the Earl of Trent. I know your father and I've come to take you from this place if you wish it."

The joy that sprang to life in her eyes was so pure he almost felt a tug at his deadened conscience to let her go.

Almost.

I'm no weak man to turn at the first obstacle. And you, my pretty little bird, have a part to play in the game ahead. Every drama needs a leading lady...

RAVEN COULDN'T BELIEVE IT. She'd been daydreaming about storm fairies and some nonsense about sprouting wings and flying away as soon as her father, the King of Clouds, realized she was there. And now a man in a top hat and a grey wool coat with jet buttons was offering to take her away. The King of Clouds had come after all!

Raven smiled and did what she'd always done.

She accepted whatever was ahead with the faith of a creature that still clung to hope.

"Well?" he asked coolly and she realized she'd failed to answer him.

"Yes! I would very much wish to go, your lordship!"

"Then we'll go." He held out his gloved hand and she took it, placing more than one forbidden toe off of the stone square and allowing him to lead her from the yard.

"Can I bring Pepper? She's five but she's very—"

"No."

Raven held her tongue, despite the hundreds of questions that began to clamor inside of her head. She had no desire to irritate her savior and decided that there would be time enough to ask about her father, or where he was taking her, or even how he had found her. As for Pepper, she was sure that there would be a better time to ask and convince him that Pepper would be no trouble at all and that Raven would happily share her food and provisions to make room.

At the outer gate, a black carriage with gold painted piping was waiting and Mrs. Hoggerty stood by the stone arch, her mouth pinched into a tight line of disapproval.

Raven lifted her chin a fraction of an inch and the instant she had one foot safely on the other side of Greenwood's locked iron gate, she risked sticking her tongue out at the woman who had tormented her for months.

But instead of the stream of curses Raven expected, the woman smiled maliciously and leaned in to whisper, "The Devil has you in hand now."

Raven blinked in surprise.

"Miss?" the coachman asked as gestured for her to climb up the step he'd unfolded from the carriage.

The interior was the sumptuous color of cherries, velvet and leather bespoke luxury she'd never seen before and the warmth of it beckoned. Raven swallowed hard. Her new benefactor was already inside and the earl leaned forward just a bit to give her a challenging look. "Are you coming? Yes or no?"

"Yes." She frowned at the way her voice sounded small and shaky but she took the coachman's hand all the same and climbed up the steps, doing her best to ignore Mrs. Hoggerty's ominous smiles and the haunting sound of her final words.

The Devil has you in hand now.

Does he?

Well, then, let's see where he takes me.

CHAPTER 1

ent

Spring, 1866

"It's expensive, that one," her maid murmured as she dutifully held up a hand mirror to allow her mistress to take another look. "As fine as any in London."

"Do you think so?" Raven tipped her chin downward to study the effect of the raspberry hued silk lining of the rim as it formed a halo against her dark curls. "Well, Lord Trent insisted that I was to have whatever I wished if it meant holding my own and not looking like a country bump when his friends arrive from London!"

Kitty said nothing and Raven pinched her playfully on her arm to evoke a small squeak of protest. "Eek! You cruel thing!"

Raven smiled. "You're meant to say how lovely I look and then something encouraging about following my heart's desires, not sit there with your lips pressed together simmering about how spoiled I am, Katherine Polk!"

The maid shook her head. "As if you needed encouragement! I've known you too long to bother. You'll buy it no matter what the cost once you realize it makes your eyes sparkle and if I point out that you'd look just as lovely with a burlap sack perched on your head, where's the challenge in that?"

They had been mistress and maid since Raven had first arrived under the Earl's roof and Raven's love for Kitty was more akin to a sister than a servant. "The challenge," she said as she turned back to adjust the bonnet to a slightly jauntier angle, "is in stopping me from buying two!"

Kitty shook her head. "Why in the world would you wish for *two?*"

"Why, so that my lovely lady's maid can have one to match and can make a certain groomsman mark her every passing!"

"Miss Wells!" It was Kitty's turn to pinch her mistress on the arm though Raven was too quick for her and darted around the milliner's counter to avoid her just punishment for bringing up the forbidden topic of the very handsome stable hand. "What did I ever do to deserve such wickedness?"

Raven laughed. "Wickedness is its own reward and if you'd rather catch his eye without the use of a feathered cap, just say so!" She turned to the milliner, Mrs. McWhorten, before Kitty could protest any further. "I'll take this one and wear it home."

"Very well, Miss Wells." Mrs. McWhorten deftly put the bonnet her customer had arrived in into a hatbox and handed it over to Kitty. "A pleasure to have your business, as always."

Raven raced from the shop without a backward glance. Her laughter rang out as she transformed into a blur of silk and feathers bursting through the milliner's doorway. Her every thought was bent toward the thrill of having visitors at Lord Trent's estates and the entertainments that would follow. Pure joy at the acquisition of meaningless frippery and the liberty of a new bonnet bestowed upon its proud owner carried a lively young Raven Wells out onto the cobblestones with the speed of a yearling.

"Miss Wells!" The cry of alarm from her maid inside the doorway came a breath too late.

The solitary rider had little opportunity to do more than attempt to avoid a collision with her colorful revelry and was rewarded with the loss of his seat. She was spared completely but he was vaulted off his mount and landed without an ounce of redeeming masculine grace on his backside on the muddy stones with a muttered groan of pain.

"Oh, sir!" Raven exclaimed and rushed toward him. "Oh, god, are you murdered?"

He closed his eyes and lifted a gloved hand to his forehead shielding most of his features from view. "No," he answered, his deep voice lowered as the breath had been knocked out of him. "Just give me a moment."

She knelt next to him, retrieving his hat, secretly admiring what a delightful sprawl he made with his broad shoulders and long lean limbs. "I can give you as many moments as you need, although if you lie in the street for too long, Mrs. McWhorten will send for the doctor." She glanced up nervously to assess how many of the villagers were already slowing their steps and staring toward the commotion she'd caused. "Should I send Kitty for him myself?"

"No." He immediately began to shift up onto his elbows. He opened sapphire blue eyes, revealing himself to be insanely attractive in face as well as form. "If I survived the fall, I suppose I can survive the humiliation of it."

"Perhaps...not many noticed your misfortune." It was a ridiculous proposal but she fought to keep a straight face as no less than three faces appeared in the milliner's windows and as many more in the dry goods store across the way.

"I'm not *that* lucky."

Raven shyly held out his topper. "You must admit it was a spectacular tumble. But you didn't break your neck and that's lucky enough."

"Oh, no!" He groaned again. "I've saved the life of an optimist." He finished sitting up, wincing as his bruised spine protested, and took the hat from her hands. "God help me."

"You aren't an optimist, I take it?" she asked doing her best to ignore the heat of a blush creeping up her cheeks.

"Never when I have muck on my backside." He shook his head and regained his feet, treating her to a rushed impression of his glorious height and strong masculine lines. He was a young man in his prime and just a few seasons shy of thirty if she had to guess. Raven liked the gold streaks in his brown hair and wild turn of its curls. He was a gentleman if she judged him by the cut of his clothes and expense of his boots. He retrieved the dropped reins of his horse who had dutifully circled back for his rider. "It's a personal philosophy of mine to adhere to a darker view when gravity has…the upper hand."

She giggled and he looked down at her still perched at his feet on the cobblestones. He held out a hand to assist her back up and she popped up like a sprite.

"If I let anything as inconsequential as mud interfere with my happiness, I wouldn't know myself," Raven said. "And nothing should interfere with a woman's happiness, don't you think?"

He released her hand slowly and took one measured step back as if to study her in amazement. "No, I can't think of a thing that should. Though I'll deny saying such a light-hearted thing if you attempt to quote me."

"I cannot quote you without giving you credit by name, sir. And as you are a stranger to me, it appears that you are safe on that account." She admired his proud demeanor and the way he wielded his masculine bluster to ward off an introduction while he still clearly felt at a disadvantage. She knew very little of men but she knew enough not to press him if he felt cornered.

"Thank God for small favors." He brushed a hand down the front of his coat, a ghost of a smile tugging at his lips. "I'll limp off with the last shred of my dignity intact."

"I would never think to rob you of that illusion," she said, deliberately looking at him through her lashes. "Oh, look, here comes the apothecary…"

Confusion knit his brows together before he caught the meaning of her words and wheeled around to accept that there was no escape.

"Sir! Sir! Are you destroyed?" The portly man was huffing as he jogged up, the enthusiasm of his concern making him red in the face. "God, what a flight that was!"

"I'm completely unharmed. Thank you for your concern." He

moved to the side of his mount to adjust the saddle. "It was a small mishap."

"Not that!" the apothecary said, exhaling in a wheeze. "A heroic disaster and won't the earl be forever in your debt for it?"

Phillip's hands froze on the leather straps and he turned back to the man, struggling not to look at the exotic vision standing innocently by the store's brick front. "The earl?"

"The Earl of Trent! You nearly killed yourself to not run over his beloved ward!" Mr. Forrester supplied before raising a hand to beg mercy while he tried to catch his breath. "God! What a commotion!"

Damn! Why am I cursed when it comes to Trent?

"You." He shifted back to face the girl. "*You* are Geoffrey's ward?"

"I am," she said brightly as if it were perfectly ordinary to meet a man after unseating him from his horse.

His breath caught in his throat. He was not a fresh-faced buck to become flummoxed at the simple sight of a pretty girl but this—this was somehow different. The village and most of its inhabitants were awash in drab colors of the earth compared to her. Porcelain features, raven black hair and eyes the color of smoke, she was an unsettling young beauty that moved without a hint of shy reserve and yet there was nothing unladylike about her.

And he'd nearly killed her.

He bowed a bit awkwardly, then regretted the custom as his bruised back protested. "Phillip Warrick, at your service."

"Raven Wells," she said and then performed a saucy curtsey in response to his gesture.

The maid's shocked gasp behind them reminded him that there'd be no rewriting history. "We were fated to meet, Miss Wells."

"What a poetic thing to say!" she exclaimed, lifting one of her gloved hands to touch her own cheek.

"Not really," he amended quickly, swallowing with grim resolve the thrill that her youthful exuberance betrayed. "I am to be a guest of the Earl of Trent and was on my way to his estate for a visit. He was kind enough to include me in his party but not apparently considerate enough to mention that…"

Words failed him as he realized the awkward turn he'd taken.

"That I exist?" she finished on his behalf. She laughed, light merry music that sent shimmering warmth through his frame.

Phillip stiffened his shoulders to try to ward off her alluring powers. He'd accepted Trent's invitation to mend the rift between them and prove to the man that he was worthy of a renewed friendship and business association. Mooning over the man's "beloved ward" was the last thing he intended!

Damn it! Stop staring at the girl and get on your horse!

"I'm sure he's not required to make an announcement of his every connection, especially to me. I barely qualify as an acquaintance."

"And yet he's included you in his rather exclusive country party," she pointed out. "But you are right. Lord Trent is very protective of his privacy and by extension it seems of mine. I, for one, shall take the omission of my name and existence as a good omen."

"An omen portending what exactly?"

"That despite all of the warnings about every event, word and whisper in a small village or great house being immediately known in the wide world, it apparently isn't true. Just think! All these years of behaving perfectly for fear that I would rend the fabric of the universe and I was anonymous all the while. An opportunity to be wicked without consequences completely lost to me!" She sighed so prettily that he nearly forgot his astonishment at what she was saying.

"Yes. Quite." It was hardly an appropriate response but Phillip couldn't think of what a man is supposed to say to pure unbridled mischief in the guise of a glorious beauty.

Her abigail cleared her throat to bring him back to the reality of a red-faced apothecary, a populated village lane and the social challenges ahead.

"Pardon me, sir, but we should be getting on with our morning errands," the maid said. "I'm sure they'll be eager to receive you at the manor house and express their thanks for my lady's safety."

Phillip nodded quickly. "Of course! I will meet you under more proper circumstances then and since I have no intentions of describing this incident, perhaps we can omit all thanks."

Raven's eyes lit with a flash of keen wit. "For a man who derides optimism, you continue to amaze, sir." She leaned forward slightly and dropped her tone conspiratorially. "I will wager you a shilling that Mrs. McWhorten's youngest is dispatched and even now hurdling his third stone wall on his way to Oakwell. The house will be abuzz with every detail of your fall before you've achieved the lane. What say you?"

"I say I'd forgotten the charms of country living."

She grinned as she straightened to take one prim step back. "Come, Kitty! We will leave Mr. Warrick to finish his journey and see if that bolt of purple silk is still set aside in Mercer's." She curtsied sweetly. "Thank you again, sir, for your chivalry on my behalf."

She retreated with her maid in tow before he could think of a clever reply and he was left to ignore the apothecary's impassioned invitations for him to sit for a while and "take a powder for his pains". Phillip waived the man off as politely as he could, remounting his horse and heading out of the village.

But not before risking one more look back at the figure in bright blues and greens who had thrown him in more ways than he'd ever dreamed possible.

CHAPTER 2

"*He* wants to see you in the library right away, miss," Mr. Walters, the butler, took her wrap but she kept a good hold on her new bonnet.

"Of course." She did her best to hurry to the library without appearing to seem rushed. It was always a balance to please the vague rules of the house and her guardian's erratic moods. Running was forbidden but so was keeping the Earl of Trent waiting a second more than he considered reasonable.

"You're back sooner than I expected." He stood from his chair the instant she crossed the threshold of his sanctuary.

Raven smiled. "Mercer's hasn't gotten in anything new since I was last in though I did land on a purple silk that pleased me. And...I was under the impression that your guests may have started to arrive."

Lord Trent nodded. "They have indeed. I take it that you met Lord Warrick?"

"Is he a lord? He did not say!"

"Did he not? How interesting! Only a baron but yes, a peer to be addressed as such," Geoffrey said dismissively. "What did he say, Raven? And how *exactly* did you meet?"

She straightened her shoulders, accustomed to Geoffrey's need for full reports. He was a very attentive guardian and while not affectionate, she took his interest in her every move as a sign of his care. "I rushed out of the milliner's without looking where I was going and the poor man fell off of his horse to avoid running me down. Kitty was beside herself and I had quite the lectures as soon as the excitement had waned." Her eyes dropped to the bonnet in her hands as she continued, "But Mr. Warrick—I meant, Sir Warrick, was unharmed except for his pride which I fear suffered a terrible blow."

"Was he surly?"

She looked up, startled at the question. "No! He was—sweet and then mortified when Mr. Bircher revealed who I was. I think he was very distressed to think how upset you would be. He said something about being fortunate to be your guest and..."

"And?"

"And made a very gallant comment about being fated to meet me." Heat flooded her cheeks and she knew there would be no hiding it. But Geoffrey had no patience for lies of omission and if he sensed there were more to the story than she was sharing, he would grind every detail from her and she would risk childlike banishment from the house party. Weeks of anticipation made such a punishment unthinkable!

"God, that's perfect!" Geoffrey exclaimed and Raven nearly started in surprise.

"Is...it?" Raven blinked. "What part of the story earned such an accolade?"

He laughed and relief flooded through her.

"I'm delighted you made a memorable impression on the man. That is all."

"Well, perhaps the cobblestones made a far more lasting impression on him than I ever could. I want to make it clear that I—behaved properly and hope you're not concerned at—"

"Raven!" He stopped her with a smile, resuming his seat and stretching out his legs. "My delight allows me no room to bother with the niceties. Besides, you've done just as I asked. You've always been attentive to your tutors, kept yourself in good order, demonstrated a weakness for fashion and for the most part, stayed out of your curmudgeonly guardian's way."

Relief coursed through her. Geoffrey's temper was mercurial but his sunnier moments were impossible not to enjoy. "You're a generous dragon and the very best of guardians! And you're the only man in England to think a weakness for fashion is a thing to be required of a woman when I'm fairly certain every female breathing will happily volunteer to drown in ribbons and silk if it is an option."

"Not *every* woman," he countered. "And I think a healthy dose of vanity suits you."

She smiled. "And to think I thought modesty was the better virtue…"

"Modesty is highly overrated," he said, adding to the jest with a wild lift of his brows. "And what does a goddess need of such camouflage? Bright feathers win the day as is proven by that bonnet. Is that your newest?"

"It is! Do you approve?" She held out the bonnet, showing off the plumage.

"Naturally." He reached out to gently touch its rim. "I want you to have the trappings of a rich heiress."

She blushed and bit the inside of her cheek to keep a nervous laugh from spoiling the moment. He was generous to a fault but recently these hints that he would settle some great amount on her were difficult to absorb. He never said as much directly but his speeches in the last few months about her appearance matching her "station", the plans for an elaborate debut season in London and an increase in every account she possessed in the village, all added to her speculation.

"Is Mr. Warrick a good friend then? That you would be so pleased if he—"

"Warrick is nothing."

Warrick is nothing? Why in the world is he delighted in me impressing a man if he is truly nothing? Raven held herself very still and waited for him to continue.

"Be yourself, Raven, and keep those feathers preened and bright. If

I require more of you, I'll let you know. Make sure you are rested this afternoon and I will see you this evening for dinner."

She curtsied respectfully and retreated, wisely swallowing her questions. She'd get her answers before long and without stirring up her guardian's ire. The mystery of the handsome Sir Warrick was a delicious challenging puzzle that snagged and tugged at her intellect but also at her heart.

* * *

PHILLIP LET out a slow silent breath and prayed that it wouldn't be interpreted as a sigh by the valet. He was one of Trent's men and as a guest, Phillip knew that every nuance of his behavior or attitude could and probably would be conveyed to his host. It was the potential price to paid for the use of another man's servants. He'd have brought his own valet but Boxwell's wife was sure to produce their first child any day now and Phillip didn't have the heart to haul a fretting heartsick manservant into the wilds of Kent. Warrick caught the valet's gaze in the mirror and tried to take his measure.

If the man was content in Lord Trent's service, he was a spy at his back. If he was ambitious or hoping for a change of placement, then he might be a potential ally. Either way, it was just one more wrinkle in the gambit ahead.

Trent had hinted that he was willing to entertain additional investors in his next scheme and Phillip was determined to win the man's trust. Trent had a knack for plucking fortunes from thin air and a reputation for hoarding the best opportunities away from his peers. Years ago, he had enjoyed a place in the earl's inner circle but a small misunderstanding had led to Phillip's banishment. Only now had he been invited to return.

All things were once again within reach.

"What do you think of the cut, Timms?" he asked.

"It flatters you, sir." The valet stepped close to smooth out the sleeves. "I took the liberty of reinforcing a seam on the left shoulder earlier. It will stand up to wear without any worry now, your lordship."

Ambitious then. Thank god.

"I hadn't noticed it. Thank you, Timms. You are a lifesaver." He turned to make it easier for the man to tie his cravat, used to the ritual of dressing. "I wish to make a good impression on Lord Trent, without any ragged seams showing."

"Fear not, sir. I am ever vigilant."

"I will rely on that," he said. "My fate rests in your hands."

Timms straightened his spine, pride infusing his expression. "I'm your man."

He wasn't but Phillip wasn't going to press the point. "I was…" Phillip cleared his throat and started again. "I was fortunate enough to be introduced to Miss Wells in the village today."

"Yes."

Not one mention of his tumble and the muddy state of his clothes when he'd arrived. Phillip couldn't help but like the manservant more for his restraint. "Is she a direct relation of the earl's?"

Timms averted his gaze as he went to select cufflinks. "It was never made clear, but there are rumors to that effect. He has a distant heir, a nephew who stands to inherit the title but we have never met the young man. As to Miss Wells, her allowance is said to be substantial and he has openly declared that her future is determined."

Phillip's pulsed jumped at the inference. If she was not related by blood, her prospects were hard to surmise but even if Trent had an heir, if the earl meant to ensure her future, then she would be in the company of some of the richest women in England even without a formal title.

Not that he was even remotely interested in pursuing her.

The memory of eyes the color of grey and silver storm clouds made the lie harder to cling to but Phillip forced it. He wasn't about to squander years of waiting for Trent to yield his icy stance for a dangerous flirtation. He'd lose the earl's approval before he had the chance to draw a breath in the man's presence.

And that was something he couldn't risk. His responsibilities and duty to his family's estates and their tenants were too great. He'd done well enough to stave off the worst but he envied Trent's financial talents.

A bell rang downstairs signaling that the guests were beginning to gather for dinner and ended their conversation. They finished the ritual and Phillip left him to take his place in the theatrical pageant of Lord Trent's drawing room.

The house was grand and elegantly laid out, and Phillip made his way down the broad staircase without a glance at the stately portraits and ornate statuaries that appointed Oakwell.

"Baron! What a pleasure to have you here!" The Earl of Trent said as he stepped forward in greeting. "It's been too long!"

"I agree." Phillip took his hand and shook it warmly. "And the cause of that delay is my only regret for—"

"I don't believe in regret. It serves no purpose a man needs. I myself have no regrets, Warrick. None." Geoffrey clapped him on the shoulder hard enough to challenge the younger man's balance briefly. "Come! Let's have a drink before dinner and introduce you to some of the other guests. Lord and Lady Morley are here as well as Mr. Sheffield, whom I was sure you knew from one of his horse clubs in Town. The party has rounded out in the last three days so it is a nice advantage to be in the first beachhead landing before the firing begins, do you not agree?"

"Yes." Phillip nodded as he put on his best game face. "Although I didn't realize there'd be pistols drawn before dinner."

Trent laughed. "There's that serious boy I remember so fondly!

The earl led him through the wooden doors into the grand sitting room and Phillip shifted into the social rhythms of introductions and subtle alliances that could make or break a house party. Mr. Sheffield was a stranger to him but it was clear that just by demonstrating a good knowledge of horses he could hold his own on the sole topic of Sheffield's interest.

Lord Morley was an older man, a starched troll of a gentleman with echoes of fashions and eras long gone to mothballs in his manners. His wife, in startling contrast, was at least thirty years his junior, a cheerful plump thing dripping with jewels, perched on a damask chair to play the hostess in the absence of any other married ladies in the group.

"Lord Warrick," she sighed after introductions had been exchanged. "Aren't you a breath of fresh air! A bachelor is as rare a find at a country house party as a live hen in a fox's den!"

"My god, Millicent! You'll make the man fear for his life!" Lord Morley said, his eyebrows arching in disapproval. "And force him to confirm that he has good sense by fleeing your cackling."

"Oh, please!" Millicent laughed. "What handsome man ever ran from a compliment?"

Phillip noted uncomfortably that Lord Morley's grip on his chair arm tightened until his knuckles shone white.

"I feel obligated to warn you that I am bound to disappoint on all counts, Lady Morley. I am a dull man these days and Lord Trent," Phillip nodded toward his host, "Only included me as a mercy to allow me to escape the dreary city for a time. I'm no suitable entertainment for any lady these days and I was assured I would suit the quiet of the country."

"You'll suit perfectly for my wife has no talent for conversation with bachelors and less apparently for being any judge of suitable entertainments," Lord Morley pronounced firmly as he gave his wife a quelling look.

"Yes, well..." Lady Morley rose from her seat and the men automatically followed suit. "If you'll forgive me, I have a sudden headache. I believe I will take my dinner upstairs, your lordship."

"Of course!" Trent said. "I'll have my butler make the arrangements. I hope you recover quickly."

"She will." Lord Morley waved his wife away and she withdrew without another word.

Trent stepped forward with a cheerful smile as the men resumed their places. "You know the way of it, Warrick. I've arranged for a few diversions, a picnic here and there or a shooting day but for the most part I expect my good guests to see to their own distractions. Dinner is at eight."

"Shall we play a round of cards tonight, gentlemen?" Lord Morley asked. "To kick things off?"

Phillip shook his head. "Not for me. I'm afraid I don't gamble."

"No?" Trent's brow furrowed, his expression one of discontented surprise. "A few years ago when we were better acquainted, you were mad for a good game."

"True enough." Phillip acknowledged the accusation. "An insanity I have had to cure myself of—and my purse has thanked me for the effort." He smiled, his tone deliberately light to diffuse Trent's disappointment.

"Never mind!" Lord Morley chimed in. "We'll have players enough for a good run and I for one, am looking forward to many nights of skilled play."

The earl's humor was slower to return but he appeared to make an effort. "Yes. Well, I hope you've warned your wife that you may leave here on foot as a pauper if I get my way."

"I'm more likely to leave with your best tapestries rolled up and tied to my carriage roof!" Lord Morley boasted.

Phillip said nothing. He was grateful that he was staying clear of it. His penchant for reckless gambling was long behind him but even if he had still played, Phillip wasn't sure it was a wise choice in light of his goals. Trent was not going to be impressed with how Phillip had changed if he fell back into the vices of his youth. And he didn't have deep enough pockets to justify the risk. *Not anymore.*

"Cards are enough entertainment for me," Lord Morley announced. "I come to the country for quiet as well, for God's sake. Not to be hovered over with contrived events."

"Careful there, old boy!" Trent pulled a brandy from the tray his footman held out. "You come to the country to prove an entertaining guest to your host. You are skating near to the edge."

There. Lord Morley looks a bit chastised at that but what a universal truth! We're here at the earl's hospitality and you have to earn your keep. Old and young.

Trent's gaze refocused on Phillip and he braced himself for the earl's attention.

"So. You aren't a lively flirt or a card player. If you tell me you don't shoot and hate riding, you may want to rethink your holiday, Warrick."

"I love to ride, shoot and a good conversation is like meat to the soul, is it not?"

Trent smiled, as jolly as if Phillip had offered to stand on his head. "Ah! There is the charming lad I had hoped to see again!"

Phillip inclined his head in a mock bow and Trent laughed. "I'm relying heavily on you, Warrick, to uphold your end!"

Three more houseguests arrived in their finery and Phillip admired the balance of the group. The earl had clearly made an effort to include some diverse personalities—no doubt again to add to his own pleasure. The elderly Mr. Carlton was the local squire and a notorious wit where his wife was as sweetly shy as a maid of fourteen despite her advanced years. Lady Violetta Baybrook rounded out their party, with fashions that echoed the turn of the century and a hawk-like countenance promising that not all would be light and laughter if she had her say.

There was still no sign of Miss Wells. Her absence should have calmed him but it was having the opposite effect. At every introduction, his eyes trailed to the door, anticipating her arrival.

He wasn't sure if he should apologize again or if she would say something in front of the others—in front of the earl. And then she was there. Another rush, a flurry of colored silk and she was among them; a bright flash of life and laughter in a room that had lacked both without realizing it.

Damn. This is going to be nearly impossible, isn't it?

She met the earl's guests with an open eager spirit, pleased to have the chance to prove to her guardian that she was equal to the role of hostess and had not wasted her tutors' time or the investment of his years of generosity.

It was all a rare treat. But here was the perfect opportunity to flex her social wings before taking full flight in London. Raven spied Phillip immediately but savored the way his eyes followed her as she slowly made her way around the room. It was heady to have captured such a man's attention. It was a rush of power, of pure sweet power.

"How lovely you look, Miss Wells! Tell me again how old are you?"

Raven's eyes widened in surprise at such a direct question but the earl had taught her that rank and title sometimes stripped its holder of the responsibility and entanglements of good manners. "I am well into my seventeenth year, Lady Baybrook, and look to turn eighteen before summer."

"But already so self-possessed! And what a beauty! My goodness, but I think the Ton will not know what to make of you!"

"Must I be made into something?" she asked innocently.

Several guests laughed at her naïve question but Phillip Warrick's gaze held steady, a glow of approval in his eyes.

Trent stepped forward. "My ward is not so easily swayed by flattery and flash. My incomparable girl will tame them before she's filled out her first dance card."

Raven blushed and Trent extended his hand toward Phillip. "Here. Come meet my ward. Sir Phillip Warrick. Miss Raven Wells."

She curtsied. "A pleasure to meet you."

The simple ritual did not allow her to linger or ask him if he'd recovered from his fall that morning. Mr. Walters rang the bell for dinner and everyone naturally moved to take their places for the procession in. Since their numbers were not yet as even as Lord Trent preferred Lord Morley graciously offered to take her in despite the break in precedence. However, no one objected since it was early days and the abrupt absence of Lord Morley's wife was softened by the polite maneuver.

Sir Warrick was placed closer to the earl's end of the table and not near enough for her to do more than pick up some of the louder side of his dinner partner, Mr. Sheffield who was very disappointed in his spring foals. Raven smiled at the scene since it was evident that it was all Sir Warrick could do to nod and express his sympathies.

Poor man. The seating arrangements are not likely to change throughout his stay and even when Lady Morley recovers—he'll still be within reach of

Mr. Sheffield's riveting opinions on Scottish hybrids versus their British counterparts.

Raven had fared better and liked the shy Mrs. Carlton and her clever husband. He was a frail gentleman but his white hair was thick and carefully curled to betray that he took some vain pride in it.

"Are you nervous about going to Town, Miss Wells?" he asked.

"You are so kind, sir. I am a little, to be honest. Everyone wishes me success but then they always add a word of warning about the consequences of failure. It's extremely daunting."

"Ah, the terrors!" Mrs. Carlton sighed. "I thought I would faint dead away in anticipation of my first ball."

Mr. Carlton lifted his glass, his eyes on his wife. "What providence it was for me, my sweet girl! It was an easy thing to sweep you off your unsteady feet and a gift to allow me to play the hero."

"Gift? You did more than play act. You were very gallant." The older woman smiled and then lowered her voice in confidence to Raven. "And he still is!"

Raven was utterly charmed. Mr. Carlton began to tell stories of London and the humble heroics that had won him the heart of his shy and dainty Mrs. Carlton. The lady demurred as best she could, clearly flattered at her husband's mythical tales and gentle compliments. Their love had frozen them in time, blinding them both to the change of years.

Every few minutes, she stole a glance at Sir Warrick's misery until he caught her at it. Raven stiffened as if an arc of electricity had bolted between them, a conspiracy of wit robbing her of breath and sending a dozen giddy butterflies skittering around her stomach. He inclined his head, a nearly unnoticeable salute to their private jest before Mr. Sheffield began to bray about a recent horse fair and Phillip was forced back to the conversation at hand.

She turned back to enter into a lively conversation with Mr. Carlton that began to touch on a classical education which Raven was happy to demonstrate.

"Did your ward just quote Durant and manage to prettily correct my Latin?" Mr. Carlton asked.

Lord Morley lifted his head, a bit aghast. "My god, what kind of education did you give this girl, Trent?"

Trent continued to slice his meat, barely stirred by the topic. "I don't remember what I told her tutors but I'm sure it was something about covering the basics." He leaned back in his chair. "Raven. What did I tell your tutors?"

"To make sure I had the education of a proper English young lady, that I could carry a tune and once that was mastered, it was up to me to fill the hours with whatever subjects I would stay awake for," she supplied with a playful smile.

"Oh!" Geoffrey perked up a bit and squinted. "How did that go?"

"I think it was six months and when I'd demonstrated a sufficient hand in watercolors, sung a few arias, made three pillows and proved I could read poetry without any ill effects, I had free rein."

"Impossible!" Lord Morley protested. "A girl in charge of her own education?"

"Are you upset because she didn't squander the chance, Morley? Or because she's better educated at the cost of pennies in comparison with whatever fortune you've squandered trying to shove your sons through their schooling?" Geoffrey teased. "Hell! I'm too frugal to complain if my ward is occupied so easily and I'm left to concentrate on my business concerns."

Raven smiled and ducked her head. Lord Trent had spoken the truth. He wished to be bothered as little as possible in the natural course of days and had once announced that he didn't care if she were studying African dirt moles so long as she made a decent feminine representation at his table.

Lord Morley shook his head, staring at Raven as if she now possessed two heads. "You have done her an unthinkable service, Trent, and there will be Hell to pay for it, mark my words!"

"I prefer to think I have stepped out on a revolutionary path and demonstrated that when you encourage a woman to follow her every impulse it leads to—" Trent stopped and made a study of his own of his ward. "Well, as you see!"

Raven's cheeks warmed in embarrassment but the moment finally passed as Mr. Carlton bravely entered the fray.

"Lord Morley, the girl has not been raised by wolves and I am sure Lord Trent exaggerates to make our evening more lively. Although, I did wonder if one or more of the boys in my schooldays hadn't been parented by badgers…"

The jest broke the tension and the dinner concluded without further incident and the ladies withdrew according to custom to leave the men to their port and cigars. The earl waved them off and Raven linked arms with Mrs. Carlton to lead the way to the blue salon.

Speculation regarding the health of Lady Morley became the first topic over glasses of sherry and Raven listened quietly.

"I hope she recovers soon! It feels wrong to enjoy ourselves with one of the party laid low," Mrs. Carlton sighed.

"Does it?" Lady Baybrook asked archly. "I fail to see why the constitution of a woman I have barely seen more than twice should influence me one way or the other."

Mrs. Carlton fell silent, unwilling to argue in the face of such blatant disregard.

"Would you like a touch more sherry, Mrs. Carlton?"

"Only if you will have a small glass."

"Oh, I do not partake. Lord Trent does not approve and says that I am too young," Raven said as she refilled Mrs. Carlton's glass. "But I am happy with the company."

"Indeed!" Lady Baybrook nodded. "Wise man," she added as she set her own empty glass down and retrieved her third serving with a deft hand. "I am relieved that despite all that nonsense about the lack of structure in your education, the man isn't completely without common sense. There is nothing more unattractive than a young girl tippling away without regard to decorum."

Mrs. Carlton politely held her tiny glass in her lap and made a study of the liquid.

An awkward silence unfolded and Raven began to silently echo her new friend's wish for Lady Morley's quick recovery since the bulk of the effort in conversation to engage the prickly Lady Baybrook now fell to her.

I'm a rabbit tethered to a wolverine.

"Tell me, Miss Wells. Trent is your guardian but what is your connection to his family?" Lady Baybrook asked.

Snap. Snarl.

"He is a generous benefactor, Lady Baybrook. I have been told very little of my noble lineage but understand that he knows my father and took me in for the sake of that friendship."

Lady Baybrook raised a single eyebrow at the words 'noble lineage'. "And your mother? Do you know anything of her?"

Her claws are razor sharp.

"I am not at liberty to say, Lady Baybrook."

"How mysterious! And somewhat intriguing! The by-product of some illicit affair, I would warrant."

Mrs. Carlton gasped, not in disapproval of Raven but mortified at Lady Baybrook's lack of sensitivity.

Raven kept her chin up, her gaze openly defiant and proud. She wasn't going to justify the woman's words or protest at being one breath away from being called a bastard. Trent had taught her better than that. He'd hammered home the lesson that only shameless icy bravado could carry you through fire. The mention of a noble parent was a deliberate move to keep people back on their heels. Raven simply waited for the old woman to wither under the weight of her own gaffe.

"Not that...I may have misspoke to..." Lady Baybrook retreated under Raven's unapologetic stare.

"I am as cherished as any daughter and blessed to reside in the earl's good graces, to have the benefits of an expensive education and the privileges of a guardian's *strict* care."

"Yes it's clear you are a very accomplished young lady. I may have overstepped, Miss Wells. I apologize."

"No need for that, Lady Baybrook. You are too esteemed to be so rude as to call the ward of *your host* out by some unthinkable slander. A woman of your grace would never trespass so thoughtlessly or mock the charitable decisions of a respected peer." Raven stood. "But I hope you'll forgive me. I am usually abed by now and find myself fading."

"Poor dear." Mrs. Carlton said as she also rose to her feet. "You're wise to rest as you can before your first season in Town for you'll soon witness more sunrises than you ever thought possible. Perhaps I should go up as well to—"

"Oh, stay! Stay, Mrs. Carlton!" Lady Baybrook commanded churlishly. "The men will rejoin us in just a few minutes and I cannot face their numbers alone. Our host is sure to accuse me of chasing all of you away!"

"Yes, yes, of course." Mrs. Carlton's courage faded and she retook her seat. "Well, good night, my dear."

"Good night, ladies." Raven retreated calmly.

She loathed interrogations and no matter what Lord Trent said, there was no amount of silk or sweet manners to prevent small-minded people from saying whatever they wished. The insulation of her life at Oakwell would not extend to completely protect her in Town. It was the earl's firm belief that his wealth and acceptance was an unquestionable barrier she could dance behind but Raven knew better.

Even so, she was determined not to fail him.

After all, what choice did she really have?

She'd reached the first landing of the main staircase when Sir Warrick spoke her name.

"Miss Wells?"

"Sir Warrick. Are the gentlemen heading into the salon? Did you lose your way, sir? It is just there down that hall if—"

"No. I'm not lost. I stepped away early to—" He caught himself before he confessed that he'd fled Mr. Sheffield's endless sermons on horse breeds. "To retire."

"It has been an eventful day." She looked down at him feeling awkwardly like Juliet on the balcony.

"Eventful meeting you twice," he said with a smile.

"Be honest. Which meeting did you prefer?"

He laughed. "I'm not going to answer that."

"No?"

"If I say it was the village, then you'll think me mad. And if I say your guardian's drawing room, then you'll think me a bore." Phillip crossed his arms. "I'll just say it was a pleasure both times, and leave it at that."

"Fair enough," she said. "Then I shall keep my own preference to myself as well."

"I should let you go upstairs. It wouldn't do for the others to catch us conversing here." Phillip took his foot off the lowest riser. "I bid you good night, Miss Wells."

"Good night, Sir Warrick." She smiled and ascended the stairs, and for the first time in her life, relished the wicked and wonderful notion that a man like Phillip Warrick might be watching her every move.

CHAPTER 3

*T*he next afternoon, luncheon was set out under the grand arch of an ancient oak, one of the many massive trees that gave Oakwell Manor its name. Within sight of the house, a long table was laid out with crystal and linens in an enchanting display that defied their shading oak to spoil the display with a single unwanted leaf.

Phillip marveled at the labor and pain it must have taken to produce such a fairy tale setting. The promenade of guests in finery in various shades of ivory made them a flock of doves or cranes landing on the scene. Lady Morley was still absent but Timms had indicated that morning while he dressed that the lady was reported to be unwell. Phillip assisted Lady Baybrook to her chair and then looked up to see Raven Wells sailing across the lawn. White lace and muslin glowed in the sunlight and she appeared like an angel to him.

However the elegant saunter of her hips quickly banished the ethereal impression. Trent's ward evoked more earthly thoughts than spiritual ones and Phillip blinked to stop himself from staring. He took one of the last empty seats as diplomatically distanced from Sheffield as he could manage.

"When do we go shooting?" Lord Morley asked over a plate piled high with pastries.

"I have a target shoot arranged in a few days, old boy," the earl announced grandly.

Raven took a lawn chair nearest to the Carltons. "Do you shoot, Mr. Carlton?"

Mr. Carlton laughed. "I can fire a weapon but every bird and woodland creature on our property has learned that the noise from my gun is no danger but merely a nuisance."

His wife nodded cheerfully. "I love to sketch them and enjoy how tame they've become thanks to my husband's terrible aim."

Lord Morley scowled. "And overly plentiful, I'd warrant! There's no husbandry if you're leaving it to predators and poachers."

"I have a good relationship with our local tradesman and when the seasons call for it they have permission to take only what they need. You see? The benefit of a gameskeeper without the hire of one and even better, not a stranger puts one toe on my land without report for the villagers guard their bounty very generously."

"A socialist and rebel in our midst, gentlemen!" Mr. Sheffield announced. "Pure ruinous nonsense!"

Raven gasped. "Mr. Sheffield! How unkind and most unfair of you!"

The earl smiled. "Defend yourself, you cruel animal!"

Sheffield's face darkened at the playful taunt. "I'll not enter into a debate and spoil the party. Especially not with one so young and obviously ill informed of the way of these things."

"Poor man." The earl placed a pastry on his own plate and tapped his glass for a servant to fill. "You leave me no choice, sir. Miss Wells, my dear. Explain your view."

"I did speak out of turn, your lordship," she began softly. "Perhaps I should apolo—"

"Explain your view, Miss Wells." Trent's tone was all command and Raven's capitulation was immediate.

"It is never nonsense to take a generous and Christian spirit in any approach and if I understood Mr. Carlton, the men he has charged with permission to hunt on his land have the restrictions to take only what they need for themselves and their families."

Sheffield chuffed disapproval. "And what is to stop them from taking whatever they can and selling it in the markets to add to their own purses?"

"Common sense, Mr. Sheffield," she answered brightly. "If they took too much game then everyone would go hungry, would they not? And since their covenant with their landlord is predicated on their respectful management of the privilege, why would they risk its revocation? Why they would, as Mr. Carlton has said, be even *more* diligent in guarding those boundaries! They would have no love of any interloper that might upset their happy arrangement and spoil the prosperity of their hamlet."

"You give the common man too much credit for good sense, Miss Wells," Mr. Sheffield said.

"And you too little," she countered. "Mr. Carlton, has anyone ever assessed the health of your game?"

Mr. Carlton nodded. "I have an inventory and report made every two years and have received great compliments on the bounteous state of all, both fish and fowl and even larger game fair well, it seems."

"The lady appears to be winning the day," Phillip said. He'd been able to take immense pleasure in watching the debate unfold. Apparently Miss Wells thrived on good arguments and the sparkle of delight in her eyes was absolutely hypnotizing.

Poor Sheffield indeed! If you weren't an idiot to begin with, I'd say this little exchange will make the title a permanent one.

"Nonsense!" Sheffield sat up straighter in his chair. "It is an aberration that cannot be replicated. I challenge you to consider what would happen if every tenant farmer and common laborer demanded the same right to 'take what he needed' with no thought to the sacred rights of his landlord? Every estate in England would be stripped bare and the chaos of revolution would bring down the very stones we have built our empire upon! The lessons of France are still fresh in my mind if not in yours, Miss Wells."

"How is it that every man of privilege whenever pressed on the subject of rights immediately reverts to some vague and frightening reference to the guillotine?" Raven's tone was as light as if they were discussing the color of the sky. "Mr. Carlton, do you fear a revolt from your tenants and tradesmen?"

"Heavens, no!" Mr. Carlton exclaimed.

Raven turned back to her opponent. "There. You see? Only tyrants fear revolt, Mr. Sheffield. If there is a crack in the stone, then there is nothing, no power on this earth that can keep it from falling apart. Time, weather and a thousand invisible forces will have their way and the strongest granite crumbles if it has a fault. That is not revolution, sir. That is science, pure and simple."

Sheffield lost his wind and busied himself cutting the meat on his plate. "Science! Hearing a woman speak of science is like hearing a cat bark!"

Phillip shook his head as Mr. Carlton and the earl openly laughed at the man's discomfort. Only Lord Morley and Lady Baybrook failed to join in the merriment.

"At least the consolation with the shooting is that we can leave the women and their endless chatter behind," Lord Morley grumbled.

Lady Baybrook opened her fan with a crisp popping sound of disapproval. "Science and politics are unattractive adornments for any true lady of good breeding."

Geoffrey's smile didn't dim but something feral and protective came into his eyes and Phillip marveled that the older woman wasn't wise enough to see it.

"Then this is a debate you and I will continue throughout your stay, Millicent," Trent said as he leaned back in his chair. "It always makes me sad to think that women in society are banished from our presence whenever we wish to converse on anything of substance. But then, I imagine it's so that the effect isn't spoiled."

"What effect is that?" Lady Baybrook demanded.

"The illusion that there is more going on in your empty heads than a silly obsession with lace."

"I am not insisting that my gender has empty heads!" she said, openly affronted. "Nor a remarked obsession with lace!"

"No? Only insisting that by avoiding more in depth conversations you need not reveal a lack in the feminine intellect? Or was is it an insistence of the attractiveness of some subjects over others for a proper woman's mental selection?" He took a sip from his glass. "What I mourn, Millicent, is that you think it off putting for a woman to display knowledge on serious matters like philosophy, science, engineering, or even politics; whereas I find it off putting to see a blank look in a woman's eyes. But then, I am notoriously eccentric, am I not?"

"To your ward's detriment, sir!" Lady Baybrook stood in a huff, forcing the men to all politely rise as well.

All rose except Lord Trent who deliberately kept his seat with a lazy shrug of his shoulders.

"There is no beauty in stupidity," he said calmly, immediately sending the dowager off in a tremendous temper across the lawn back toward the house.

"That was a bit harsh, sir!" Lord Morley commented wryly as he sat back down. "So much for the quiet of a country visit."

"I apologize, friends," Geoffrey offered. "I have always encouraged my ward's educational pursuits and cheerful views. She will be the match of any man. So the fault is mine, not Raven's."

Sheffield shifted on his cushions. "Not that I am raising my hand for another serving, but Miss Wells may regret your lax attitudes come this social season. Not everyone is as receptive to an over-educated woman as...we are."

"No? You do not think there are enough simpering milk-toast debutantes in our little world to satisfy them? Must every woman be cut of the same cloth?" Lord Trent asked, then stretched his arms out to take in the day. "But what say you, Warrick? Milk toast or meat? Which do you prefer?"

Phillip nearly choked on a piece of mutton he had just put in his mouth as everyone's attention was immediately directed toward him.

It took him a moment to recover but at last he could respond. "I loathe your analogy, sir."

"Yes, yes." Trent waived the complaint off. "How do you like your women best? Shy, insipid and demure? Or something more clever and self aware?"

It was stupid to look toward Raven. Stupid. But also impossible to avoid. For there she was, as beautiful as any woman he had ever beheld, openly clever and quick. And those smoke colored eyes looked directly back at him without apology. This was no biddable maiden bred to be ruled. She was a feminine creature crafted to rule and he was more than half way to succumbing to her spell.

"Intelligence is never a fault and in a woman when it is balanced with compassion and her better nature, it is irresistible."

"Ha! See? You cannot over-educate a woman! Though you can certainly under-educate them if you insist on the taste of soggy milk toast!" Trent pounded on the table.

Raven sighed and finally re-entered the fray. "Let us change directions! To make amends for the somber turn in our conversation, I propose a diversion."

"What kind of diversion?" Mrs. Carlton asked.

"Something that may please both sides of the table—a scavenger hunt!" she said.

"What?" Lord Morley's brow furrowed. "It is a game for children."

"Not the game I have in mind," Raven said. "Let us see if I cannot come up with a list of items for the search with clues that can entice you to think differently of the enterprise. I will engineer a hunt that the ladies can pursue as well so that no one is left out!"

"I do love a good game." Mr. Carlton chimed in cheerfully, adding to her supporters.

"Who doesn't love solving a mystery?" Phillip admitted.

"Please allow me to orchestrate a grand game to make up for the mischief of the day. I will take some time to come up with my scheme and get everything in place and then we can start." Raven looked to the earl. "Do you approve?"

"I do! And if someone prefers to sit out the game and forfeit their chance at the prize, then so be it."

"What prize?" Sheffield asked.

Trent smiled enigmatically. "Are you playing then?"

"I might."

"Then if you win, you'll find out," Trent said and clapped his hands in triumph.

"Give me until tomorrow to arrange all, gentlemen!" Raven said.

"And the prize to the winner?" Sheffield pressed again.

"Is not the boast of victory sweet enough?" Mrs. Carlton asked.

Lord Morley scowled. "If you expect a man to gad about like a chimpanzee after insipid clues, it is not!"

Some of Raven's enthusiasm wavered but Lord Trent intervened smoothly. "What a crusty damper you are, Morley! If it distracts the women of the house in looking forward to the game and gives us the rest of the day to blessed peace to play cards or do as we wish undisturbed, then how can you not rally to the notion?"

Lord Morley rolled his eyes in disgust. "God, party games!"

"Oh, don't be such a spoilsport! No one is making you play." The earl stretched out his legs. "I think it's a novel idea."

"I will see to everything!" Raven stood and once again, the men moved to politely echo the maneuver by rising; this time with the earl also participating as he rose from his chair. "If you'll excuse me, I have quite a bit to do."

Her excitement was palpable and Phillip admired the deft way she had effortlessly shifted the group's mood to a happy turn. In an elegant flurry of skirts, she left them and Phillip forgot not to stare at her beautiful hurried retreat.

* * *

RAVEN HAD to reach up to place a hand on her bonnet for fear of it flying off at the pace she set back to Oakwell Manor. The luncheon had been a near disaster thanks to her tendencies to speak too directly but the earl seemed pleased with her (even if Lady Baybrook was most

39

decidedly not). Even better, Phillip Warrick had revealed that he might also approve of her wit and that was a new thrill she had no desire to forego.

The scavenger hunt had been a stroke of inspiration. She would mend the bonds of their party with a bit of silly fun and prove to all, perhaps even Mr. Sheffield that she was not a revolutionary of any kind—rather a peacemaker.

And inspire Mr. Warrick to continue to look at me with that heat filled intensity that makes my bones feel hollow?

It was no small undertaking but Raven was determined to contribute to the party's entertainment. As she gained the house's main entry, she picked up her skirts and raced up the stairs. Ideas for clues and the wonderful twists of the quest ahead chased through her head and Raven began to hum to herself in delight.

Even prickly and curmudgeonly company was compelling after so many years of semi-isolation. She had no friends her own age since the earl dictated that he preferred for her to have as few "country" associations as possible. Even her ventures into the village to shop provided only momentary relief. She always felt like an outsider looking at the lives of others, admiring their families and friendships. But her undefined social position made alliances difficult and none of the locals had attempted to cross the lines of formal conversation toward casual warmth for fear of offending Lord Trent.

As she reached the first floor, she hesitated.

Lady Morley.

Thoughts of her own loneliness pushed her to recall that there was a guest under Lord Trent's roof who may be suffering from the very same malady. "Poor lady," she sighed. "Missing dinner and then our outing—a setting she can probably see from her bedroom window while we laugh and cavort without a thought to her comforts!"

Raven turned to head down the hall toward the Jade bedroom which she knew the Morleys had been assigned. It was one of the manor's best with a lovely vantage and when the house was largely unoccupied her favorite room to hide away to read a forbidden novel. She decided it would be a good secret to share with Lady Morley to form a friendship if the opportunity arose. Raven knocked on the door and awaited her welcome.

But there was none.

At last a faint sound like a muffled cry came through the door and Raven's instincts recoiled in alarm. Was she truly ill? There'd been no word of sending for a doctor. Had her maid left her unattended? Was she in distress? Without hesitation, she turned the latch to open the door a few inches. "Lady Morley? Pardon the intrusion but I…"

At first glance, the bedroom was empty but the stillness was broken by a single solitary figure in a dressing gown sitting at the vanity. A trifold mirror betrayed the woman's state in three glorious angles and Raven's blood turned to ice.

Her eye was cruelly bruised and her upper lip was swollen from the violence of another blow. Lady Morley's eyes widened as she realized her privacy had been violated and she came unsteadily to her feet, raw horror in her expression.

"Please go!"

Raven started to retreat, numb and unsure of herself but then stopped. "Can I send for a doctor? Or—"

"No! My husband would be furious if I…made a fuss. Please." Lady Morley's composure began to crumble. "It's my own fault for… I made him angry. Please say nothing."

"As you wish but…I will say nothing to anyone else. Although—"

"Swear it. Swear you will tell no one what you've seen!" she said, an edge of desperation cutting into Raven's soul.

It was all she could do to nod her assent. "I swear it."

And then Raven ran from the room, with every light hearted spirit she'd known swallowed by the chasm of pain at her back.

CHAPTER 4

*G*eoffrey walked back toward the house with Phillip as the rest of the group broke up to spend the afternoon as they wished. Sheffield had headed toward the stables to make what he could of the earl's animals and no doubt formulate his suggestions for where improvements could be made. Lord Morley had mumbled something about resting before dinner and the Carltons had strolled off holding hands into the manicured wilderness that extended off from the crushed gravel pathways.

"What do you think of it all so far, Warrick?"

Phillip smiled. "I think if I stay out of the fray, I'm bound to have a very lively and entertaining time of it."

"Wise man," Trent said with a chuckle. "Though I confess, I didn't remember Morley as being such a crab. But he was always good at the tables and I invited him with an eye to making sure you had a skilled opponent. What a misfire!"

"I'm sorry for it. Gambling was well and good when I had extreme youth to blame but when the IOU's outweighed my purse, I just couldn't be that fool anymore."

"Have you recovered financially then?" Geoffrey asked with keen interest.

"I have, though I would be content with more of a cushion against any unseen turns in my fortunes."

Geoffrey deliberately let the statement go, aware of how painful it was for any man to beg. He'd lured Warrick in with hints of a new investment scheme, already guessing that the younger man needed more capital, but to hear it was nothing short of a delicious thrill.

"But Sheffield! What an ass!" Geoffrey exclaimed. "It doesn't take a seer to predict that he and that bulldog faced Lady Baybrook will be making their excuses before the week is out!"

"You never know. Sheffield may decide it is his duty to convince you all of his brilliance after that luncheon. And while this is my first meeting with Lady Baybrook, I suspect she never leaves the field of battle without being carried off."

"Good eyes, Phillip! We'll push through and win them back. Sheffield has money to burn and can help me keep Morley at bay and Millicent may yet settle down and get some enjoyment in providing my Raven some guidance with the gift of her experience. In her day, Millicent was the toast of London and I had hoped for better stories from her."

"She may just need some gentle prodding."

"I'll assign that task to you then. Tame the old bird and see if she can remember how to smile."

"I'll do my best."

"You always did have a talent for bringing a woman to heel." The words tasted like bile in his mouth. *God*, he hated Warrick. Smug in his youth, Geoffrey saw only arrogance and ignorant spite that could justify the sins of his past. *I took you under my wing, Warrick. And for my generosity, you repaid me with treachery as you helped yourself to the banquets in my home, the benefits of my company and the favors of my mistress's bed!*

Of course, it was that last trespass that had set all in motion and Geoffrey smiled at the simplicity of his plans for revenge. Warrick had stolen from him like a child and received no punishment. So the lesson had gone unlearned. He had failed as a mentor to demonstrate to his charge the natural course of things but now, he would set things right.

Warrick would learn. He would learn that there was a price to be paid for every wrong.

"Enough! We're too clever to stand about and flatter each other's prowess, sir. Only fools need to preen," Geoffrey said firmly. "And I am no fool!" He brushed off his coat and stepped back.

"No, and only a fool would mistake you for one," Phillip said. "I'm off to see about exploring your library. Would you care to join me, your lordship?"

Geoffrey shook his head. "I'll pass. My pride in the collection extends only as far as its hefty monetary value. It's only my ward who becomes dreamy eyed over those dusty tomes. Perhaps you should ask her for a tour."

Phillip's expression was hard to read but Geoffrey knew where his thoughts would turn.

Trying to imagine that lovely creature reclined with a book in her hands, or flirting with you over a few open pages, dear boy?

"Well, I shall leave you to manage. Time enough to talk business." Geoffrey touched his hat and left Phillip without another word. His mood improved as he turned back toward the gardens to the east of the house.

It was as if God Himself was on his side and Geoffrey was more than happy to give the Maker a good view of one of the best games ever played.

PHILLIP SIGHED and continued on toward the house's main entrance. He was making slow progress with Lord Trent but it was progress all the same. At least he'd gained the man's favor again and the earl was as friendly as they'd ever been. But asking Raven Wells for a private introduction to her guardian's library seemed a dangerous undertaking fraught with peril.

She was a beauty. There was no denying it. Phillip accepted that he would be wiser to do his best to avoid her in the next few days. He'd already made too much of a show of her effect on him as Mr. Carlton had whispered to him when he rose to leave, "Watch yourself, young sir. I had that same look on my face when I spotted my wife at her first dance and I have never lost it in all the years since."

Lucky man.

But let's see if a delightful conversation or two with the 'charming' Lady Baybrook doesn't cure me of every romantic notion I've ever had... and remind me that I'm not here to fall in love.

* * *

GEOFFREY WALKED the paths of his gardens without really glancing at a single plant, his mind mapping paths of vengeance without any attention to his feet.

"Your Lordship?" Raven's voice interrupted his reverie and he turned, surprised to find her back outside.

"I thought you'd bolted in to work on your scavenger hunt." Geoffrey looked around her, curious to note if Warrick had driven her out. "What goes then?"

"It is—Lady Morley. I am breaking a promise but I fear for her. I think her husband has...injured her...and..." Her voice was unnaturally halting and unsure and her lack of confidence irritated him.

He held up a hand to stop her. "What nonsense! A married woman's tears are as much a cause for concern as the color of the sky. Mind your step, girl, and see that you change your dress before tea is served. I confess I was boasting to Lady Baybrook about your talents for pretty turns."

"How can you be so callous? So cruel?"

"Oh, was I?" Geoffrey said, genuinely startled at the notion. "I am a practical man, Raven. Who can fathom the inner-workings of the private and inviolate fortress of someone else's marriage? You are young, my dearest. I'm sure you'll choose more wisely than Millicent when it is your time and every happiness awaits you in a good match. When some delightfully rich man has won your hand, what further worry could you have?"

"Surely marriage is based on more than coin, Lord Trent."

"Is it?" He shrugged his shoulders, nonplussed. "Perhaps in novels, but what do I know? A confirmed bachelor speaking of marriage makes me a pigeon advising a lioness how to hunt. When that tasty gazelle comes by, feel free to use those claws, my lovely."

She sighed. "And Lady Morley?"

"I will say nothing and shield the woman from knowing that you have failed to keep your promise. If there is one thing no one appreciates, it is a person who lacks integrity, dearest. No worries! Your misstep goes no further and we won't speak of this again." He smiled, pleased at the simple solutions that life provided and continued down the path.

RAVEN RACED up to her room, shaking off the disquieting affect of Trent's notoriously convoluted metaphors. Her plea for Lady Morley's safety had gained her nothing but a strange serving of natural and bloodthirsty images from the African plains. Even so, she knew better than to push any harder. He'd made his position clear enough and Raven didn't want to risk one of his darker moods.

There would be no support from her guardian if she interfered with Lady Morley.

Since when has that ever stopped me from doing as I wish?

"Kitty, did Lady Morley bring her own lady's maid?"

"She did. A trim and tidy woman by the name of Mrs. Lindstrom." Kitty said as she began to pull out dresses for her mistress to choose for dinner, along with the next day's selections.

"Do you get on with her downstairs?"

Kitty shrugged. "Well, enough. She's a bit of a tight-lipped creature but courteous enough."

"Was there...any mention of Lady Morley being unwell?" Raven pressed.

"Only in passing. Walters said she'd complained of a headache but when Mrs. Keller asked if Mrs. Lindstrom required a headache powder for the lady, it was refused. John thought it strange but I told him if my mistress suffered headaches often enough, any maid worth her salt would pack her own powders and remedies." Kitty held up a blue dress with velvet piping. "For dinner?"

Raven nodded without even looking at it. "Yes."

"What are you up to?"

"I am not up to anything." Raven crossed to her writing desk. "I have a scavenger hunt to organize and a great deal on my mind." She took out a few sheets of paper but abandoned them, too agitated to consider sitting down. "I think I'll go downstairs to ask Mrs. Keller personally if she doesn't mind me asking the staff for a bit of help with the game."

"I can take her a message if you'd rather."

"No. I don't mind and I want to make sure that my silly diversion doesn't create any fuss if everyone is already overworked."

"As you wish, miss." Kitty said and then began to pull out a day dress. "Here, let's get you changed for the afternoon and—"

Raven balked at the delay. "Must I?"

Kitty's entire demeanor changed as she slowly turned back to study her mistress with new eyes. "Out with it."

"What?"

"Not in all the years I've known you have you ever hesitated to happily change your frock and glowed at the prospect, Raven Wells. Not once!"

"There is always a first instance, Kitty. Not that I am accepting your claim. I'm sure I'm not such a shallow thing!" Raven crossed her arms, then immediately regretted it since it only made her look like a petulant child.

"Out with it."

Raven weighed it all out before she spoke. She'd made a promise to say nothing but the threat to Lady Morley's health felt far heavier. "I need to ascertain if Mrs. Lindstrom is the ally of her mistress or more loyal to Lord Morley. I need to discern where her sympathies lie."

Kitty's face tightened in confusion. "Is there a rift between the pair? If so, then I can tell you plain, no servant will betray such a thing or make the mistake of choosing any side that might put them out of a position. Such is the way of it, Miss Wells."

"It is more than a rift."

It took a few seconds but Kitty's expression softened. "How badly is she hurt?"

"Badly enough that I don't think we'll see her at dinner for at least another day or two." Raven dropped her arms, all pretense at bravado gone. "Will you help me?"

Kitty nodded, her lips pressed into a thin line of disapproval. "I'll do what I can. But you can't be burning the man alive with hateful looks at dinner!"

"Easier said than done," Raven confessed.

"You say one word or make one sniff at Lord Morley and he'll blame his wife for throwing herself on your mercy. He'll punish her all the worse and leave this house with his wife bundled screaming under his arm; and then what will you have to say for yourself? You'll have done more harm than good and disgraced the earl!" Kitty said firmly and then retrieved the saffron colored day dress from the bed. "Change your dress for the afternoon and trust me to see to it at the servant's dinner tonight. I'll give you a full report when I come up to help you to bed."

"Very well."

The ritual of changing was a welcome distraction. The layers to be shed, the new layers added, it was a choreographed dance between mistress and maid. The bright yellow set off Raven's coloring and even with the anxiety of the day's discovery, her mood lifted a little. She watched Kitty in the mirror and lifted her long hair to keep it out of the way of the maid's nimble fingers. "Do the servants talk, Kitty? Downstairs. I mean, how open is their gossip and manner?"

"You know they do! It is understood that there will be gossip to be shared or hoarded almost like currency."

"Like currency," she echoed in fascination.

Kitty went on, encouraged. "Think of it like a secret mirror beneath your feet. The same layers of class and hierarchy but on a lesser scale, guarded with the same zeal and fraught with some of the same political dangers."

"As above..." Raven whispered.

Kitty nodded. "So it is below."

She eyed Kitty from a fresh vantage point. For here, standing in grey muslin and a white apron, was her counterpart and her reflection to the "world below". She had new respect for her maid.

It's power, too, isn't it? I never paid any mind before but I think I should have.

As the door closed behind Kitty, Raven took her seat at her desk and forced her mind to turn to the scavenger hunt. Joy had drained from the day but her obligations remained. She'd promised them all a grand puzzle and there was no reneging now. She lifted her pen and began to write out the list of items for the players to seek along with the clues and assignments that she would hide throughout the house and gardens in the grey of pre-dawn. She made sure that each player's list included a few unique items to keep it exciting.

Even so, her mind wandered. The thrill of a house party and the romance of a London social season had lost most of its glitter after one look at Lady Morley. Trent implied that Raven's judgment would be more sound when it came to choosing a husband, but something in her rebelled at the notion that Lady Morley had willingly partnered with a monster.

More likely Lord Morley was as sweet as sugared pears when they met...

Raven wasn't sure marriage was quite the "prize" she'd been led to believe but as for considering herself as some predator—it felt ridiculous.

Sir Warrick has no resemblance at all to a creature that one would "take down"—but he stirs something in me that wonders what the chase would really be like if a man like that were at my heels.

Or if I were in pursuit of him if that's truly how it works.

She glanced out the window at the oaks and recalled the look in Phillip Warrick's eyes; and then boldly added a final item to the list with his name on it.

Lady Morley may not be the only one in need of an ally, or of comfort.

CHAPTER 5

The day of the scavenger hunt dawned as Raven knew it must. She'd been working on the lists, in between her subtle efforts to see to Lady Morley's state and make a bright show of cheer at dinner to hide her concerns. Kitty had engineered what she could below stairs and before bed, a brief note from Lady Morley to Raven had expressed gratitude along with another plea for her discretion.

A sleepless night had yielded to morning and Raven prayed that subtlety was a skill that one could acquire by hoping for it. "Good morning, all!" she greeted the room breezily. Her forced smile gave way to genuine surprise as she spotted Lady Morley sitting next to her husband at the table.

"Ah! Here is my ward!" Geoffrey said. "Raven, this is Lady Morley who we missed at dinner."

Raven curtsied and took her seat. "A pleasure to meet you at last, your ladyship."

"A delight," the woman returned softly. "I was just telling the earl how we've looked forward to this holiday."

Raven did her very best not to stare at the faint shadow of a bruise on the woman's face camouflaged by powders. Kitty's ointments had done wonders for the injury to her lip. *Thank God.* "Oakwell Manor is known as quite the haven from the city."

"Yes, well...my silly luck to catch a cold just after we'd arrived!" she exclaimed. "My poor husband has been left to fend for himself but I will do my best make up for any lost time."

Lord Morley smiled. "Millicent is far better at social nonsense than I."

"God, what woman isn't!" Trent said with a laugh. "Well, I am glad to see you recovered, dear lady. What a bear he's been without you!"

Raven kept her eyes on her plate. If she didn't know better, she'd have believed every word and seen no sign of trouble.

Mrs. Carlton poured herself another cup of tea. "Will you be joining us in the game, Lady Morley?"

"Game?" Millicent asked, openly confused.

"There's to be a ridiculous scavenger hunt after breakfast," Sheffield grumbled. "It was Miss Well's doing."

Raven blushed. "I do not have a list for you, Lady Morley, but if you wish to partner with someone?"

"Oh, please feel free to take my place!" Lady Baybrook said. "My knees already ache just considering all the scurrying about and unnatural excitement of the thing."

Lady Morley glanced at her husband who nodded his approval.

"Yes, I would enjoy the diversion! What fun!" Millicent said.

"Very well, everyone who wishes to participate will meet in the library for your lists at ten." Raven warmed to the subject. "You will have until three in the afternoon to get as many items on your list as you can. We shall meet there and see who is the champion of the day."

"And if there is a tie?" Sheffield asked.

"Then the clock will decide," Trent intervened. "I'll position myself in the library later and make a note of the time of your arrivals. Lady Baybrook may join me if she wishes to act as my lieutenant. If two of you have the same number of tokens, then whoever checks in earlier will gain the advantage."

Mr. Sheffield nodded. "That seems fair."

"It is more than fair," Trent said with the authority of a man long used to having the last word. "I should also add that anyone who fails to reach the library by three will forfeit the game, even if they have achieved every item on their list."

Phillip smiled. "I can see my strategy coming together."

"It is nearly ten now, so if you'll excuse me," Raven said as she pushed back her chair to stand. "I shall gather the lists and see you in the library."

She left to do as she'd promised but also to have a brief word with Kitty who was waiting in Raven's bedroom.

"How did she appear, Miss Wells?" Kitty asked.

"You knew she would be out?"

Kitty shrugged. "Mrs. Lindstrom said as much after we'd finished the morning's dressing and preparations. Lindstrom said she was real grateful for the help of the salve and I gave her the recipe in case..."

"In case Lady Morley ever has need of it again?" Raven asked with a sigh.

"Oh, it's certain to come to hand, sooner or later. But Lindstrom's given me the nod and I think I'll be the first to know if she decides she wants a friend." Kitty held out the lists, each folded and sealed, from Raven's writing desk. "Nothing to be done for it presently. So here. Enjoy the day!"

Raven took the papers nervously. "I may do just that. Thank you."

She hurried back downstairs to the library where the group awaited their assignments. Phillip Warrick was present and one look at how handsome he appeared leaning against one of the carved columns near the section on histories made her question her sanity.

"Let's have them then!" Mr. Sheffield barked. "The sooner we start, the sooner I have the prize in hand. No offense, ladies, but I fail to see how the odds can favor you in what is sure to become a foot race."

Raven didn't bother answering him directly, a smile tugging at her lips at the realization that the man who'd protested the scavenger hunt the loudest was now its most eager player. "Here, we are. Please don't open your lists until after the clock has chimed." She started handing each person the folded lists with their name on the outside of it, above the black wax seal she'd borrowed from the earl's desk.

"Everyone's quest is unique, so no use trying to cheat by stalking your opponents."

"I'm looking forward to this," Mr. Warrick admitted and held out his hand.

She nearly hesitated but it was too late to change course. "Good luck, sir."

"Thank you."

The clock chimed and all the guests unfolded their extensive lists to read them with smiles and gasps.

Mrs. Carlton clapped her hands in delight. "Oh, what fun!"

Mr. Carlton nodded. "I am enamored of the day ahead! Come, let's be off and may the best man win!"

"Or woman!" Lady Morley added, her humor more apparent in her husband's absence.

"That's the spirit," Raven said.

Everyone quickly moved to begin the hunt with one notable exception. Phillip read the first few items on his list and nearly laughed. It was a masterful scavenger hunt and he immediately grasped that there was nothing indolent or simple to be found. If he'd planned on lazily picking up a few things and strolling to victory, the shape of his day altered quickly.

"Item No. 4: First Earl of Trent's eyes are cast upon it."

Portrait gallery? First I have to locate the dusty boy's painting and then figure out if he is looking at something in the portrait itself or does his gaze lead to an object nearby...God, I'm having fun already.

He realized the other players were having similar experiences as they quickly sought to thank the mistress of the game before they left the library. Phillip waited until they were all gone before he stepped up to her. "It's a clever list, Miss Wells."

"Oh! Do—do you think so?" She blushed, suddenly shy with him. "Well, I...shall let you run your race then, sir." She retreated quickly and he watched her go in astonishment. She'd saucily stood over him on a cobbled street and then debated men three times her age with the self-possessed confidence of a duchess, yet now she blushed and ran.

Phillip sighed at the puzzle and decided the only cure was to do as she bid. "Very well, let's run our race." He unfolded his list again and studied it more thoroughly, starting to group the items to save himself some steps and—

Item number thirty leapt off the page and his breath caught in his throat.

Mystery solved.

PHILLIP DELIBERATELY COLLECTED several other items before he approached the gazebo. He did not want to look like an overeager schoolboy but he would be damned if he would ignore her invitation. He walked into the garden, dazed at the dreamlike sight of Miss Raven Wells perched on the cushioned bench inside.

She stood as he came up the steps, suddenly shy. "You came."

"You were in doubt?" He smiled and held up his list. "I can't think of a reason short of Armageddon that would have kept me from seeing if I can claim number thirty."

She smiled. "Ah, what a compliment!"

"I could have professed something about my competitive nature driving me here." He shook out the small paper and read the item in question aloud. "A kiss from the girl in the gazebo."

"The girl. That isn't very specific. It could have been a scullery maid," she said mischeivously. "What if I had recruited Lady Baybrook? Would you look so cheerful then?"

"What do you think?" He came up the last step and stood before her.

"I think…" She pressed her fingers against the blaze creeping up her cheeks. "You must have the most brazen impression of me. That this idea was…"

"Tell me."

Raven looked up into his face and suddenly, her words were a tumble as the truth yielded to his kind expression. "I am not fast. You see, I'm to debut in London and there is nothing to say that it won't be an unmitigated disaster. Especially since few things are ever as glorious as one hopes but I thought—I have so little to say over anything. But a kiss—a first kiss. I wanted to have a say, Mr. Warrick. And rather than risk some unwanted mishap or leave it up to an irascible and unreliable fate, what if I asked you? And as you are, I think, the most strikingly handsome man I have ever seen…"

"I see."

"Do you? Life is not nearly as predictable as I keep hoping. But if you would oblige me in this, I would be very grateful." Raven finished her case and then was torn between a prayer that the earth would swallow her whole to escape the embarrassing moment and the fervent wish that the man would hurry up and be done with it.

Just lean over and press your mouth against mine and I will be a woman kissed, at last!

Mr. Phillip Warrick shifted forward to pull her into his arms and Raven nearly squeaked in happy delight that it would be the latter. Though she immediately realized that whatever awkward event she'd envisioned was not in the offering.

One of his hands reached up to cradle the back of her head, gently tipping her back until there was nothing for her to do but instinctively cling to the man or risk losing her balance. Raven's heart pounded as she succumbed to the delicious sensation of falling into a man's arms, the heat of him surrounding her. Slowly, reverently, he lowered his mouth toward hers, until his breath was intermingled with hers and a shiver ran down her spine.

The first touch was as soft as velvet, as he deliberately pulled his lips across hers to map the sensitive contours of her mouth before he tasted her. What she'd seen as a dry and fleeting gesture evaporated in the reality of fleshly reality when Phillip Warrick's tongue lightly trailed over the plump rise of her lower lip. She gasped at the unexpected turns of strangeness that shifted to pleasure, each touch of his mouth beckoning hers to follow and mirror him in the exchange.

Raven drank in the lessons, yielding without repaying him with anything more than sighs until the eager student mastered herself. When her mouth opened to his, the last invisible threads of passive restraint broke and Raven dared to match him. She wanted to not only be kissed, but to kiss.

Bold hands moved up his back, exploring the textures of a man's shoulders until her fingers reached upward to sample the rough silk of his hair and the smooth heat of his skin. She had asked for a taste of independence and instead had been served a feast of heady surrender.

Phillip's reaction was a delicious shudder, his embrace tightening as the woman in his arms came to life against him. From maidenly stillness to hungry temptress, Raven's kisses possessed a magic all their own. She did not retreat but instead spurred him on, driving him with a heady mixture of innocence and raw sensuality. He was in awe of the discovery of her powers, so potent and intoxicating, he didn't know if he would ever be the same.

Her tongue danced against his, and every nerve ending in his body began to ricochet fire and ice. The warm wet confines of her mouth were open to him and a primal need unfurled at the invitation. His cock stiffened against the indifferent confines of his breeches and Phillip was forced to acknowledge that while obliging a lady with a first kiss was all well and good; shagging an earl's virgin ward in his garden was not going to fly.

Phillip straightened, gently kissing her until the very last instant when he was sure she was back on her feet and capable of standing.

"Oh, my!" She pushed away with the greatest reluctance freed to recover what she could of her wits. "That…"

"What say you, Raven Wells?" he asked.

"I say you may cross item number thirty off of your list, sir and that…" She blinked like a cub stepping out from its den for the first time. "I never thought to find kissing so…"

His eyes gleamed with triumph, manly pride only adding to his appeal. "So?" he prompted playfully.

"Transforming." She looked up at him, desire and vulnerability warring in her eyes.

His expression changed, a new intensity seizing them both at her confession. "Yes, it was."

"Mr. Warrick." She smoothed the curls from her face. "I rely on your discretion."

"You have it."

It was all she could do to nod. Raven was sure that if she looked down she would see her toes curled on the edge of some great precipice. For there was not a thread of refusal in her and that discovery shocked her more than anything else. In every novel she had read, a first kiss always led to a protest and an arousal of maidenly modesty that ensured that the hero would hold a reverent distance afterward.

She searched every corner of her heart and mind in a single breath and found no hint of fear, no trace of caution and absolutely nothing resembling maidenly modesty. If Phillip Warrick asked her at this moment to drop every stitch of her clothing, Raven acknowledged that she would turn away only to ask him to help her with the buttons.

How remarkable to discover that I am a wanton and unworthy thing, after all!

"You must get back to the hunt, Mr. Warrick."

A small flash of confusion crossed his brow. "It feels strange to kiss as we did and then be sent off like a schoolboy."

She gasped. "No! I am..." Heat rushed into her cheeks and Raven knew her blushes betrayed her. "I'm afraid that if you don't go, I will ask you for another and another and... This is not at all what I expected! I am asking you to go so that I can talk myself into behaving and if you are any kind of gentleman, you will leave so that I have some hope of it."

He grew very still but then finally nodded his assent, turning to leave without another word. Raven watched in helpless wonder at the retreating figure and prayed that no matter what else the day held, there would be no more startling demonstrations of Mr. Warrick's inspiring kisses. She sat down unsteadily with a long ragged sigh.

Raven Wells, after all this time, I think the Storm King has finally arrived.

And God help me, I want it to rain.

CHAPTER 6

*P*hillip stood at the edge of the gathering in the library, determined to appear composed. After kissing Raven in the gazebo, he'd failed to add a single item to his quest. Hell, after kissing Raven, he was ready to forfeit everything he had, much less the victory of a scavenger hunt. Even the promise of one of Trent's fortune making ventures now seemed useless and unappealing.

It was Raven he wanted. There was no denying it. She was beautiful and lively, impassioned and outspoken. If her dowry was as sizable as he suspected, then even without a flawless pedigree, his family couldn't object to his choice. She was everything he'd hoped for and more.

Since when did I even dare dream to find a woman with that kind of fire? She's as polished as a gemstone but there is nothing cold about Raven Wells. And god knows that kind of warmth makes even the most dutiful match a miracle.

The question was, how do you honorably win a woman under her guardian's roof without trespassing and evoking the man's wrath?

"The winner of the day is," the earl paused for dramatic effect before continuing, "Mrs. Carlton!"

The woman glowed with shy pride as her husband applauded merrily. "I can hardly credit it!"

Mr. Carlton kissed her on the cheek. "There's my girl! I glanced at her list and she was forced to question no less than ten strangers throughout the estate to achieve her victory!"

Raven smiled. "Some of my favorite souls inhabiting Oakwell, as I hoped it would prove to have been a courageous and empowering day for you. Did you like item number eight, Mrs. Carlton?"

"Oh, yes! What a delight!"

Lady Morley applauded as well. "It was the best day for me, even with victory denied! I feel positively giddy after this! I can scarcely credit that Miss Wells had time to secret away so many delightful clues!"

"A labor of love," Raven admitted. "And the maids helped me this morning, so I cannot really claim all credit."

"I swear, I feel like dancing!" Lady Morley laughed and held out a handful of red ribbons she'd collected during her quest like a child at May Day.

Geoffrey handed Millicent back her list. "As well you could! It was an admirable effort."

Sheffield took back his list with far less grace. "If my watch hadn't been set incorrectly, I'd have had it. I had two more items secured than any of you!"

"But failed to return to the library before the clock had struck three, sir," the earl said. "Stop pouting, Sheffield!" He cleared his throat as he pulled a small wrapped package from his pocket. "It falls to me to provide the prize. Mrs. Carlton, here you are!"

Mrs. Carlton took it from his hands as everyone except Mr. Sheffield celebrated.

"Open it, dearest!" Mr. Carlton urged.

The paper gave away easily and she lifted the framed miniature painting free to gasps of admiration. "Oh, it's lovely!" she exclaimed.

"The painting is worthless, but the frame is solid gold and a very pretty antique," Trent said. "Think of it as a trinket to commemorate the day."

Mrs. Carlton held up the small painting and ornate frame for all to see and Phillip watched Raven's color change slightly. Curiosity forced him to give up his place against the wall to draw closer. The painting was a delicate thing recognizably portraying the same mighty oak that they had picnicked under on the estate grounds. Bright colors and dappled sunlight hinted at a summer's day and Phillip leaned in to note the initials of the picture's author.

"R.W.?" He looked toward Raven. "Miss Wells, is this your work?"

"A trifle," she admitted. "My feeble attempt at art after failing miserably at squibbling flowers onto teacups." She pressed her hands together, her voice edged in a cheer that failed to touch her eyes. "As Lord Trent has said, it is a worthless thing."

Mrs. Carlton's eyes widened. "Not worthless! It has even greater value to me, Miss Wells, I can assure you! I am in love with your little painting and each time I view it I will remember our holiday here and your lovely company."

"Assuredly it will hold a place of great honor in our home, Miss Wells," Mr. Carlton added quickly. "The earl is too familiar with your talents to make such a judgment."

Phillip nodded, swallowing a lump in his throat at the hurt Raven was graciously denying. "I am wishing I'd put more effort into winning now that I see the prize, Miss Wells."

"Oh, good God!" Lord Trent rolled his eyes. "She isn't Rembrandt! It's an oil painting of a tree and I'm not heartless! Come, Raven. Reassure our guests that you are happy to see a sweet ending to the game."

Raven renewed her efforts and Phillip marveled at the change. With a small lift in her shoulders, she instantly embodied an airy gladness that lightened the room. "It could not have a better home than yours and the earl is right. What use is it here when we are blessed to enjoy the sight of the oak that inspired it each and every day? This way, you have a memento of your visit unique to Oakwell Manor." She reached out to touch Mrs. Carlton's hand, "And when you see it, you can summon the bravery of the day, don't you think?"

"I shall!" Mrs. Carlton said and then kissed Raven's cheek. "What a treasure you are!"

Lady Baybrook's expression remained purposefully neutral. "I for one prefer the rewards of good conversation over willy-nilly exertions that result in nothing more than a need for a long nap."

Lord Trent smiled. "My gift for entertaining conversation is impossible to rival! But on that note of wisdom, let us each retreat to some quiet pursuit before the evening unfurls. I for one, sense a long night of cards ahead. Warn your husband, Lady Morley. I am in the mood to win."

"Yes. Though my husband hates to lose so perhaps it is you who needs the warning," Millicent said then made her farewells as the rest of the party began to do the same.

Phillip watched Raven with fascination as the girl who could draw every eye with a single gesture now successfully faded to retreat from the room without much notice. He'd have said it was impossible for Miss Wells to enter or escape any room without creating a stir. But she was an enchantress with more tricks than he knew...

And he was set on learning all of them.

"You all right?" the maid asked as Raven came into her bedroom.

"I'm fine, Kitty. Why wouldn't I be?" Raven inwardly cringed at how defensive she sounded.

"Heard he passed your painting off to the Carltons," Kitty said as she began arranging the jars on the vanity.

"Gracious! How did you hear of such a thing and so quickly?"

"I think everyone's tracking things a bit keener during this holiday. But if you must know," Kitty explained sweetly, "one of the footmen made quite a fuss over it when he was bringing his tray back down and I overheard him on the stairs."

"Perfect," she sighed.

"Wasn't that the painting you made Lord Trent for his birthday last year?"

Raven shrugged her shoulders, a study in affected nonchalance. "Yes. But Lord Trent has hundreds of masterpieces in the house. It's not as if a man of exquisite taste is expected to wax poetic over an amateur scrap of canvas." She leaned against one of the bedposts. "Besides, it really was a lovely choice for Mrs. Carlton. I'm happy for her to have it. Truly."

"Truly?"

"Yes. I may have been surprised to see it at first but, I'm... completely thrilled at the gift." She crossed her arms. "Delighted, in fact."

"I'll take your word for it." Kitty began to ready things for her mistress to rest for a while as custom dictated. "Did the scavenger hunt go well?

Raven's spirits lifted at the question. "It was glorious! It was —magical!"

"As good as that?"

Raven turned so that Kitty could help her out of her day dress. "Everyone had a lovely time and I think I have redeemed myself entirely with Mr. Sheffield."

"You weren't so far into the weeds as that, Miss," Kitty said. "I'm just pleased to see Lady Morley out and about to take part."

"It was one of the best parts of the day. She looked so...happy." Raven's joy hiccupped at the notion. "How is that even possible, Kitty? Do you think anyone could experience joy in the midst of—I don't even know how to describe her challenges!"

"Even if she can't remember what happy looks like, it's the nature of a well bred woman to make a good show of it."

Raven stepped out her skirts. "She deserves more than a show."

"Show is about all anyone can hope for," Kitty shook her head sadly. "My ma always says if you hope for more, you're bound to end up with less."

"I cannot help but believe that happiness is the natural state that we all strive for and inherently deserve." Raven stroked the silk of her bed curtains and traced the embroidered vines with her fingertips.

"Strive, well enough but I'm not sure it's a real thing. Maybe in fleeting moments, but to be happy? All the time? Is that even possible?" Kitty sighed. "To bed with you!"

Raven pressed her lips together to prevent the impulsive protest of a spoiled child of fortune. Her life had been a carousel of great joy and abject misery so what logic did she think to outline that decreed a firm hold on happiness? She eyed her maid and tried another tactic as she yielded to the command and climbed into her bedding. "Do you want to be happy, Kitty?"

Kitty straightened her spine. "I don't look to dance a jig. I'm content enough and that's enough."

"Is it?" Raven dropped her hands. "I suppose that's the safer course."

She didn't need to walk to the windows and look down to know that the view included a glimpse of the gazebo's pergola peeking above the curving groves in the garden. Phillip's obliging kisses had ignited her soul with promises and transformed her into a creature edged in want and craving. She wanted more. More of him, more of the joy of his touch and more of the glorious ruin of forbidden heat.

Raven knew the rules of polite society—better than most as she skirted its edges, striving to be above reproach and beyond judgment. But Phillip Warrick had skewed all with a kiss and she was fighting to see where balance might give way to her raw need to be loved.

"You are the happiest person I have ever met," Kitty said. "It is a marvel to all who know you."

"Why a marvel?"

"Because you make it look so effortless. Because you are the only one I know who celebrates everything from your favorite jam appearing at the breakfast table to the miraculous existence of rain puddles." Kitty laughed.

"You make me sound like a simpleton."

"Then I am sorry. I meant it as a compliment, not an insult. You are too clever and well you know it!"

Raven sighed. "It's just…"

"Out with it. What is all this about happiness? Has someone said something unkind?"

"No. I was merely wondering what price I would pay to be truly happy. If it were…offered."

"What would you give to be happy, Miss Wells?"

"Everything." Raven tasted the word and accepted the weight of its meaning. "I would give anything and everything I had, Kitty."

"Oh, my!" Kitty finished smoothing out her covers. "That's quite a price to pay."

"Is it?"

Kitty crossed her arms. "No one can offer you such a thing. You have it already and if they're peddling happiness, you keep a tight hold on your purse. My ma always said it's a tear-streaked face that thinks to get heaven for a penny."

"For the record, your mother should write these things down."

"Can't write more than a simple mark for her name," Kitty began to retreat from the room. "But I'll pass along the compliment to her. Now you take a nap like a proper little lady! The earl won't be pleased to see you yawning at dinner."

Kitty closed the door behind her and Raven closed her eyes to consider the day.

She'd asked him for a kiss. Because she'd felt so uncertain of herself after seeing the pain in Lady Morley's eyes. Marriage had always been a grand and noble goal and the highest achievement she could hope for, but never had that path appeared to hold physical danger or heartless cruelty. Now she'd looked again and uncovered stories of the horrifying pitfalls of a tragic matches and miserable women in the clutches of an institution that did not provide much mercy if a husband proved a brute.

So, she'd set on the notion that it might be better to seize a little slice of control, to experience tenderness to banish her fears. If he had bruised her, her experiment would have solidified her worst suspicions about the opposite sex and eliminated all desire for a match. But his kisses had provided so much more than the simple reassurance that not all men were created equally.

Here was a happiness she had never reached for.

But there was a price for such things.

She knew now that there would be no half measures. The risk was real. Women who asked for kisses could be accused of all manner of wanton lapses in their judgment. Mr. Warrick may even now have decided that she was hardly an angelic candidate for London's lofty circles. He may have boasted to the other men of his encounter or— *God, if he's told the earl I am finished!*

Her head swam with terror.

I could plead some kind of ignorance and swear it was all a silly game.

I could.

But I won't.

Raven opened her eyes to study the ornate patterns pressed into the metal ceiling tiles above her bed. Fear was not a familiar sensation and she dismissed it quickly. "Mr. Warrick has never betrayed any sign of not being a gentleman. Only a ninny jumps from a building that isn't on fire."

It was Phillip who had ended their embrace and set boundaries. If he'd done otherwise, the debate in her head would flow differently but of all the lessons of the day, she decided that Phillip Warrick's honor was without reproach.

The conventions were clear. If a girl "set her cap" for a man, she must tread carefully. If her pursuit was a clumsy and obvious thing and she failed to win the man's heart, she would become an object of derision and pity. But Raven knew that subtle maneuvers were not her forte. Over and over her tutors had noted that she had never mastered anything at a walk. Raven preferred to run, with the wind in her face and skirts flying out behind.

Why would love be any different?

Raven smiled at the simple logic of her heart's desires.

She would do her best to behave, to please her guardian and hold her own, but she would win Phillip Warrick if she could and seize her chance for happiness with both hands.

CHAPTER 7

"*I* have an announcement, friends." Lord Trent tapped his glass as he stood from the head of the dinner table. "My ward has been the sole source of entertainments to our party so far and I find I could not be outdone. The annual spring dance at a neighbor of ours looks to be cancelled at the last because of a house fire. No lives lost though that will set the Snows back financially for a generation or two. In any case, I have received an urgent request to host the event to prevent the worst."

"The worst?" Mr. Sheffield echoed, his voice tinged with sarcasm. "Oh, yes. Heaven forbid the local gentry is deprived of the chance to prance and bounce about in circles…"

The rest of the party's reactions were immediate and varied, but Mr. Warrick looked only at her with the promise of a waltz in his gaze.

"Dear God!" Lord Morley barked. "What a nightmare!"

"Not so bad as that," Mr. Carlton said with a smile. "Country dances are the most charming affairs."

"They certainly are!" Lady Baybrook chimed in. "There is nothing untoward in the activity. And despite what Mr. Sheffield indicates, no one bounces!"

"So our small country party will give way for a single night of revelry to the county's finest families. If nothing else, the punch will be strong and plentiful," Lord Trent said. "I cannot recall the last time I made use of my ballroom. One night of dancing will not destroy your health, Morley, and just think of the card game you could arrange, sir."

"Cards?" Lord Morley cheered up instantly. "It would be pleasant to have a few new faces at the table."

"When is this grand favor to occur?" Lady Baybrook asked.

"This Saturday." Trent sat back down. "I've already sent word that Oakwell Manor would serve."

Four days. Raven's eyes widened in shock. She'd known vaguely of the local ball but since her attendance was always forbidden in preceding years, it was not an event she'd allowed herself to dwell on. Now, it was coming to her doorstep and she was giddy with anticipation. *Unless...* "May I attend the dance, your lordship?" she asked.

"Of course!" Trent smiled. "You are now of an age to enjoy such things and since I am the hero of the county for my generosity, why should my ward not expect to be the belle of the ball?"

Raven blushed, her mind immediately reeling through the dresses she had on hand for the occasion. "Thank you, Lord Trent!"

"You are most welcome, my dear."

"Will it be your first ball?" Mrs. Carlton asked.

Raven nodded. "It will indeed. I had dance tutors, naturally, but... what a pleasant surprise to find that I have only days to wait instead of weeks! I long for it all."

"Such enthusiasm!" Mr. Carlton said. "Your confidence and beauty make you a credit to the earl's house."

"She is a treasure," the earl conceded cheerfully. "I've kept her fairly hidden from the local young bucks but let's watch them strut about and make fools of themselves to try to win her."

Raven risked a quick glance at Phillip, immediately thrilled to see the somber dark expression on his face. *He is jealous to think of me dancing with other young men.*

"I see you scowling over there!" Geoffrey said with a smile. "You're not out of it, sir! A bachelor has no chance of clinging to the walls—not if he hopes to survive the night!"

Lady Baybrook nodded. "It is an unthinkable slight for a bachelor to leave the local beauties without a partner. There is always a shortage of eligible men at these gatherings and I have heard of men earning a cold shoulder in Town if they offend the wrong families with their overhanded reluctance to dance."

"Dear God!" Mr. Sheffield exclaimed in horror. "I am a wretched dancer!"

There was laughter around the table as poor Mr. Sheffield looked around in confusion. "Perhaps I should claim to have suffered an injury?"

"There's no hiding, sir," Geoffrey teased. "But have no fear! Stand with me and I'll defend you to the last."

Phillip kept his head down unwilling to give his host a better target for merriment. The prospect of a dance would normally have set him firmly in Sheffield's camp proclaiming his misery and seeking the best escape attainable. But the tantalizing notion of waltzing with Raven and holding her in his arms was extremely appealing.

What was not appealing was the equally present threat of watching Raven in the arms of anyone else.

Damn it. There has to be a way to navigate this without calling out every boy in the county who thinks to prance across from her in a reel.

And exactly when did I lose my mind and turn into a possessive ape?

He looked up from the gold pattern on his china plate to spot Raven looking at him, the storm in her eyes a perfect reflection of his. Her tongue darted out to nervously touch her lower lip and Phillip dropped his fork with a loud clang against his plate as his body surged with unspeakable heat, his cock stiffening between his legs.

All eyes diverted to him in that instant and Phillip was grateful to the heavens for the discretion of a long tablecloth and the cut of his pants.

"Courage, there." Lord Trent lifted his wine glass. "No man ever died from enduring a quadrille, Warrick!"

"Thank the gods for that." Phillip said with a sigh and won more laughter from the table.

The conversation continued, excitement and anticipation of the ball overtaking the quiet of the evening. The Earl of Trent was in rare form, his mood effervescent as he began to tell wild tales of some of the local personalities. "Can you picture it? So this farmer wakes up after a bit of home brew and swears that he's had an epiphany to make his fortune selling local mud in jars as a cure-all to the ladies of London!"

Mr. Sheffield tapped his glass for one of the footmen to refill it. "A clear example of the effects of a brain fever."

Trent waved the comment off to gleefully reach the meat of his story. "Imagine my shock when he presents himself on my doorstep clutching a dirty little vial of his concoction and demands a tour of Oakwell Manor! For you see, with the massive wealth he was about to acquire with 'Dr. Mudd's Magical Elixir', he expected to make me an offer on the house and take up residence within the year!"

"My God!" Lord Morley's disgust made his voice thick. "Did you beat him from your doorway with a horsewhip?"

"Of course not," the earl said with a wry grin. "I gave him the grandest and most thorough tour of the house that has ever been offered; including an inventory of the silver and an admonition to make sure that he have a good long look at the storerooms."

"You didn't!" Lady Morley said, her eyes wide.

"The man was practically jigging down the lane by the time I sent him on his way," Trent said.

"You ruined him with that generous show," Phillip said. "Poor man."

"And that offer to buy you out?" Mr. Sheffield asked.

"Strangely enough, it never came." The earl sighed sarcastically. "I cannot see how bottles of mud could fail to make one rich, can you?"

"It depends," Phillip said. "I've seen fortunes made on more ridiculous schemes. Perhaps in other more skilled hands?"

"Ah! There you have it!" The earl laughed. "I will be sure to consider Dr. Mudd's Magical Elixir for my next venture!"

Lady Baybrook cleared her throat. "And on that note, I believe it is time for the ladies to withdraw and leave the men to determine the details of their grand financial plans. Though I should warn you," she said as she stood, forcing the others to follow suit, "the ladies of London will peel you like grapes if you wiggle bottles of horse manure under their noses."

The comment was so unexpected that everyone laughed until there were tears. It was a chaotic retreat for the ladies but Raven marveled that even the most somber matron could provide a silly reprieve. She followed the women out, sparing one last peek at Phillip, accepting that she already thought of him as hers.

THE WOMEN SETTLED in to the salon taking their seats according to rank and Raven dutifully waited until the others were placed before selecting the seat furthest away from the fireplace.

"I want to thank you again, Miss Wells, for the day and for your welcome." Lady Morley rearranged her skirts as she sat down. "Lord Morley admitted that after hearing about the game, even he regretted missing it."

"Did he?" Raven blinked in shock.

"He never did!" Lady Baybrook scoffed. "That man would no more gad about in a party game than a donkey would pull the queen's carriage!"

"I may have stretched the truth a bit," Lady Morley admitted without a shred of shame in her voice. "Well, I had a lovely time of it! Counting stair steps and finding those pretty little red bows tied to the chandaliers—it was a thrilling chase!"

"Then it was worth it, your ladyship," Raven said. "To see you happy."

"It has been a very pleasant holiday," Mrs. Carlton added. "And now a country dance? Mr. Carlton has quite the gleam of nostalgia about him as a result."

"I cannot remember being so cheered at word of a ball," Lady

Morley said. "But then it is always fun to see romance take hold and matches made."

"In my day," Lady Baybrook said warming to the topic. "If one could spot the match being made then it was a sure sign of poor manners! Not like these days where everyone makes such a show of their attachments! It is a sad erosion of the upper class."

Mrs. Carlton pressed her lips together and studied the sherry in her glass.

"Though here at least, I can make my contribution to the night's success. My matchmaking talents are famous," Lady Baybrook went on. "I have a keen eye for the best matches and have been responsible for more honorable alliances than not. More than one family in the county may be glad of my attendance and attention during the evening if I apply my talents."

"Oh!" Mrs. Carlton took a sip from her glass to steady her nerves. "H-how generous of you!"

Lady Morley looked at Raven. "What say you, Miss Wells? Will you be content to have Lady Baybrook see if she cannot make an intro-duction or two for you?"

Raven's skin chilled at the flash of disapproval in the dowager's eyes. "There is no need. My ambitions for the night extend only as far as being present, Lady Morley. It will be a delight to see the fashions and enjoy the music."

"Such humble expectations!" Lady Morley protested.

"Miss Wells is wise beyond her years," the dowager proclaimed. "She recognizes the extraordinary generosity of her guardian in including her and knows better than to overstep."

Millicent's confusion was obvious. "Knows better? How can a single toe of that girl overstep when she is so young and beautiful?"

"You are too kind, Lady Morley. I'm sure Lady Baybrook meant to compliment me on my intention to be on my best behavior and do nothing to embarrass my dear Lord Trent." Raven smiled. "I think it will be invaluable practice before my first ball in Town this fall."

"Well, I will be happy to note which man steps up to take Miss

Wells' first dance," Lady Morley sighed. "Though I suspect I can guess who it will be."

"What? Who?" Mrs. Carlton asked.

Raven forced herself to be very still, alarm keeping pace with the blush creeping up her face. "Yes, who would you be thinking of, your ladyship?"

"It's obvious, isn't it?" Millicent said. "Why, Mr. Sheffield, of course! That man nearly fell out of his chair when there was a mention of dancing, I just knew it was his nerves betraying him."

Mrs. Carlton shook her head. "The man has done nothing but nip at her heels, Lady Morley. I hate to be the one to contradict your theory, but he has been most unkind to our Raven."

"Then it's certain he is probably smitten! Men are notoriously contrary when it comes to matter of the heart." Lady Morley's voice rang with quiet authority. "The ones that make the greatest show of protest and disapproval are always the first to fall."

Raven felt faint with relief but managed to nod. "I would never have foreseen it."

Mrs. Carlton continued to shake her head. "I still cannot see it!"

"Have you decided what you will wear, Lady Morley?" Raven asked and was rewarded as the topic changed to the dramatic improvisations of wardrobes packed for a country holiday that now unexpectedly included a formal ball.

Raven sipped her cider with a slice of sugared orange floating in it, quietly keeping clear of the flow of the conversation. Lady Baybrook's insinuations about Raven's ineligibility had not missed their mark. She had been months away from facing her fears in London. But the earl's announcement had pushed everything up and Raven was no fool. The local gentry would be polite to their host and vicariously to his ward but that may not extend as far as risking their children in an unsavory association with a girl without legitimate family.

Even so, she'd run into the teeth of it with her head held high.

Her bravery, however, was starting to lose steam. The anonymity of being one more pretty girl in a crowded London ballroom had felt vaguely possible but it was not something she was in the mood to test so soon. Not with Phillip Warrick's eyes on her at the ball if the earl's contemporaries felt as Lady Baybrook did… She waited until there was an appropriate lull in the conversation and then quietly excused herself to avoid the return of the men.

She craved another encounter with Phillip and longed to prove that the exchange in the gazebo was not a unique or fleeting experience, but she didn't trust herself to sit unmoved while he was nearby. Lord Trent missed nothing when it came to her and she wasn't ready for his interrogation.

Not yet.

Why is it that when it comes to Phillip, I have the sinking sensation that I will never be ready for what lies ahead?

CHAPTER 8

The following morning, Raven stopped in the library to pick up another book for her bed stand. She'd only just settled on what she hoped would be a distracting read to help her sleep better when she heard footsteps behind her.

She turned with a smile thinking Phillip had found her again only to realize it was Lord Morley. He was wearing his riding clothes but she couldn't tell whether he was fresh from a ride or just heading out. In either case, the sight of him no matter what he was wearing was enough to jar her senses and bring her to her feet.

"Lord Morley! Are you…"

"Miss Wells. I would normally ask what you are reading but in your case, I find the idea fills me with trepidation."

"Why, Lord Morley? Are you afraid that it may be something wholly inappropriate?" Raven said as she held out the book toward him. "I will disappoint you when you see that it is a study of the history of the Celts."

"Perhaps. Though from what I've encountered in you, I would recommend you avoid everything to do with rebellion lest some portion of that treatise on those savages inspire you to play the harridan." Lord Morley kept his hands behind his back. "Women need not read of battles."

Raven squared her shoulders, determined to hold her own but also to give no offense to a guest of the manor. "I will set it aside while you are here, sir."

He shifted his stance, studying her. "I am glad to find you alone."

"Are you?"

"I wanted to speak to you as directly as possible and it seems I have my chance."

"On what subject, sir?"

"On the matter of my wife."

Raven was sure her heart's rhythm changed and a trickle of icy fear tumbled down her back. "Your wife? Why would you wish to talk to me about your wife, your lordship?"

"I cannot help but suspect that you have formed a friendship with Millicent."

"Suspect? An odd word choice when it comes to the natural alliance of women during a country party." Raven kept the hold on her book deliberately gentle so that nothing in her carriage would give away the wariness that had gripped her. "What do you fear?"

"I fear nothing." His eyes were cold. "Millicent is like a child in many ways and enjoys your silly games and diversions. Well and good. But I do not approve of the way Trent has given you free rein. You will not speak as you did at that picnic in front of my wife. I will not have you thoughtlessly spewing your opinions as an infant vomits porridge."

"I'm not sure I understand, sir. Is it the nature of my opinions that offends you so? Or that I possess a mind of my own?" Raven lifted her chin.

Lord Morley stared at her, aghast. "It is this attitude you will refrain from displaying in her presence!"

"Do you fear that I will set some kind of perverse example for your wife?" Raven asked calmly. "Surely Lady Morley is a woman grown and not prone to paying the slightest attention to the conversation of an ill-behaved girl."

"No woman of quality would!" he growled.

"Then you should feel nothing but relief!" she sighed as if the matter were happily settled.

"You steer clear of me and mine, Raven Wells!" Lord Morley took a menacing step toward her but Raven didn't flinch.

"Yes, your lordship. As the law dictates, your wife is yours to rule." Raven matched his move with one of her own and pressed the book in her hands squarely against his chest. "But you must bear in mind, I am not any man's to rule and if you think to command me, you're a fool."

"How dare you!"

Raven stepped back and curtsied. "I will naturally do as you wish, Lord Morley, and be the meekest version of myself in your wife's presence."

His mouth fell open at her unexpected capitulation and the sight of a very innocent and yielding girl looking at him contritely through lashes the color of blackest soot. The shift was so fast, he could barely fathom it. "You…called me a fool."

"I? No! I said if you thought to overstep with me, then that would make you a fool. But you are no fool, sir. Are you not?"

"Trent should beat you within an inch of your life."

She looked up at him aware of the void at her feet. Her mistake in taunting him clanged against her ribcage. *All that rage, and he can't touch me. But, oh god…his wife will be within reach and I may have condemned her to the worst of it.* "Please." Tears filled her eyes and she allowed her very genuine fear to show. "I reacted poorly to your request because—I thought you were mocking me! Your wife dislikes me, sir and for you to forbid a friendship seemed…cruel."

"Millicent dislikes you?" he asked.

"As you do! I've made an abysmal showing and…." Her voice hitched and she put a hand to her throat. "I will say no more."

Lord Morley nodded, a gleam of satisfaction in his eyes. "See that you don't and I will not share this exchange with your guardian."

"Thank you, your lordship."

"Ah! There you are, Morley!" The earl hailed from the doorway. "We are set to mount up, man!"

"Of course." Lord Morley turned stiffly and headed toward the earl. "I spotted your ward and lingered to thank her for amusing Millicent with that game yesterday. It was a good tonic after her cold."

"Yes, yes, Raven is a delight. Come on, man! We've gotten Sheffield up in the saddle so there's no time to waste." The earl saluted Raven with his riding crop and smartly turned to lead his guest out.

She waited until she heard the front door close behind them before she raced up to her room to ring for Kitty.

Within minutes, Kitty was there. "It's early to change, mistress, but what may I do for you?"

"You must tell Mrs. Lindstrom to find Lady Morley immediately and tell her that if her husband questions her, she is to express nothing but dislike for me. He is unhappy at any hint of a friendship between us and I...may have angered him when he confronted me on the topic. Kitty, she must be warned and prepared!"

"Oh, my!" Kitty sighed. "Where is he now?"

"Off for a ride with the other men, so there is no time to waste."

"I'll see to it but please, miss. Between a husband and wife, there is no place for you to be caught meddling!"

"Yes. Brilliant advice. Thank you, Kitty." Raven crossed her arms. "Now, go and do as you are bid. Mrs. Lindstrom will have to be the messenger as quickly as she can."

Kitty nodded and left on her urgent errand.

Raven sat down at her vanity table and tried to absorb the developments of her afternoon. She'd intended nothing more than being a supportive soul during Lady Morley's stay. Clearly Millicent's husband wasn't open to any such casual connections...

Raven looked at her reflection in the mirror and weighed out her choices.

Obedience and retreat as Lord Morley wished.

Only if that is what Lady Morley truly wishes.

She did not know the lady's mind well enough to hazard a guess.

"Well, that," she announced to an approving mirror, "is something I will rectify. And if the lady desires an ally in truth, then so be it! A few books on the art of war may be just what my education is lacking."

AFTER LUNCH, she waited for the men to return from their ride and approached the earl in his study before he retired to his rooms to rest and change for dinner.

"Raven? Why do you look so glum?"

"I am sorry to intrude on your day, but I fear I may have failed to show restraint and allowed my temper to get the better of me today." Raven held her place just inside the doorway.

"What have I taught you about restraint?"

"Very little." Raven's brow furrowed, truly concentrating on the puzzle. "That it serves only at tea parties and social gatherings."

"And otherwise?"

"Otherwise I should trust my instincts and rein in my impulses only when they might cause true harm. You said it was a mark of intelligence to be bold where others are cautious." Raven touched her forehead to cool her temples. "Frankly, it is the one lesson you have repeated so often I wonder that you did not carve it over my doorway. "I should be bold when others are cautious."

"Good girl."

"Your lordship?" Raven smoothed out her skirts. "I have the distinct impression that boldness is not often associated with 'goodness' when it comes to the fairer sex. I tend to anger your more conservative friends. But…"

"Never fear the natural order of things, my dear. And if we carry this analogy forward, then real men are hunters and far more likely to admire a tigress over some paralyzed timid warthog."

Raven smiled. "I see. Well, when you put it that way, it is hard to see the appeal of a warthog to anyone."

"You know I hate women who simper. I always have. Is it any wonder that I should strive to instill in you a fearlessness that others in your sex lack? They may not always admit it, Raven, but every woman around you brims with envy at your courage of character. Ignore them. Life is short. You must seize what pleasures you can in this wretched world and demand your full measure."

She nodded. Lord Trent was warming to the familiar topic, his voice rising and the cadence increasing with his passions. Whenever he was like this, she knew that the time for true debate was gone. His ecstatic conversations were often entertaining, but they could easily turn to fury or despair. Her guardian's moods were as changeable as the weather, and his emotional storms just as violent.

"Is it unconventional? Yes! But what a priceless gift to you, girl! What need we of useless rules? Conventions are a tool in your hands, not a prison! Do you see the difference? The smallest and wildest animal is free to rely on their instincts. You are meant to be free, aren't you, dearest? Free to follow your heart and your passions? For if humans are superior to dumb beasts, then why would we have fewer freedoms? Why would we enjoy less?"

Raven blinked. He was veering close to the edge of mania and she dreaded it. "Fear not, Lord Trent. I will be bold where others are cautious."

He looked back at her, his expression slightly surprised as if he'd forgotten his audience. "Yes, yes. Go. Go and for god sakes, at dinner I expect to see you in those ruby and diamond hairpins I bought you."

"Oh," Raven stood quickly, grateful for her dismissal but slightly confused. "I thought you wished me to save them for London."

His lips pressed together in a tight line of disapproval. "Don't be stupid. If ever you were going to appear like a wealthy heiress, it is now, Raven. What the hell good are those jewels doing in some dull cupboard? Shine, girl, shine!"

She dropped her head in submission but then caught herself. He hated simpering females. Raven lifted her chin and gave him a saucy smile as she curtsied. "I will blind everyone at dinner with my display, sir."

"That's my girl! There she is!" Trent beamed, clapping his hands. "My daring little duchess!"

Raven retreated from his study at a good pace, hoping he interpreted the speed as her eagerness to please and not her desire to flee him while his mood held. Years in his company had given her enough practice in the art of strategic withdrawals to last a lifetime. But she knew that he meant well and was a victim of his passions. Poor man, she thought, it is probably why he has never married as that sharp wit and uneven temperament has likely frightened off more than one "simpering female" in his path.

Perhaps I will challenge Lady Baybrook to apply her talents for matchmaking to Lord Trent. Even if she fails, it might be entertaining to watch things unfold...

CHAPTER 9

*P*hillip was disappointed not to see her the next morning. The previous night, she'd dazzled in a red gown with rubies in her dark hair and he'd struggled to hold his own. It had been two days since he'd kissed her in the gazebo and there'd been no opportunity to find her alone since then. He was wracking his brain to think of an excuse to change places with Mr. Carlton at dinner or to invite her on some innocent outing without the older women catching his scent.

He'd finally landed on a scheme to offer to teach her to play cards or chess after the meal but he'd missed his chance to speak to her. The dry tenor of male conversation had grated against his nerves and he'd tried not to count the endless minutes before the earl finally finished his port and signaled the return to the salon where the ladies awaited them. Only to be greeted by Raven's absence and the conveyance of her polite apologies for her retreat to her guardian by way of Mrs. Carlton.

Not that he'd expected to be able to say very much with so many witnesses in attendance. The earl was in a grand mood but it would have evaporated if Phillip weren't careful.

To appease Sheffield and put on a good face, he'd agreed to a bridge game though not to any betting. Despite everything, he'd stayed up far too late. As a result, he'd missed breakfast entirely and wasn't sure where any of the other guests had gone for the day. The days were passing too quickly and a new desperation was starting to seep into his thoughts. Phillip walked the estate aimlessly and then wandered back toward the house in his best attempt at a casual search for Raven that wouldn't look like a search. One of the footmen gave him a strange look when he recrossed the foyer for the third time and Phillip accepted defeat.

So much for my career as a spy!

"May I direct you somewhere, sir?"

It was too late to lie to preserve his dignity. "I was wondering where Miss Wells could be found?"

To the footman's credit, his expression didn't change. "She is commonly found in the solarium at this time of the day, Mr. Warrick. It's the third door past the blue salon."

"Thank you."

Phillip made his way down the hallway and found the door open to a room that obviously occupied the corner of the manor facing southeast. A wall of windows created a bright oasis that looked out over a carefully landscaped miniature orchard. The room was arranged for conversations amidst wrought iron racks of ornate plants and broad leafy ferns. Phillip stepped in to see if she had selected one of the padded seats but Raven was nowhere to be found.

He raked his fingers through his hair. "This is ridiculous."

"Pardon?"

He wheeled toward the sound of her voice, amazed to discover that she was on the floor in the corner sitting amidst several embroidered Japanese-style cushions; a book of poetry in her hands. He blinked at the vision of Raven Wells with skirts the color of red sea coral pooled around her like a fairy queen sitting on a lily pad. Never in his life had he seen a woman sit so provocatively on the floor, an exotic pasha eschewing the nonsense of western chairs.

It had never occurred to him to look down when he'd come in.

"I meant...that I felt..."

Before he could hold out his hand, she gracefully rose from the cushions unaided, a smile on her face. "You have come upon me in one of my favorite hiding spots, Mr. Warrick."

He eyed the emerald green silk cushions on the ground. "Miss Wells. Do you ever do or say anything expected?"

"Of course not. What would be purpose?" she answered with a smile. "Besides from all that I've read, most men don't expect a woman to do much of anything beyond the limits of their imaginations so why bother trying to be predictable?"

"Miss Wells." He stepped closer and lost his train of thought.

"Yes?"

"Who are you hiding from?"

"Must I choose only one? I think it might be Lady Baybrook." She leaned in with a mischievous smile. "I have the distinct impression that she longs to rap my knuckles with her fan."

The scent of her hair and her skin permeated his senses and the bloom of familiar heat spread throughout his frame. Kissing her again was inevitable. "I don't think you are a child to be punished."

"No. But I fear I can be naughty all the same."

Damn it. His body tightened instantly and Phillip had to shift his weight to make sure his coat was shielding his state from her view. She was already so close that pulling her into his arms would have been as effortless as taking a breath. "Miss Wells. You have an amazing gift for saying the most unpredictable things."

"So I have been told." Raven studied him for a moment. "Do you still have an aversion to optimism, Mr. Warrick?"

"It has faded considerably."

"Has it?"

"Truth be told, your company could make an undertaker smile, Miss Wells."

"You weren't all that sour to begin with, sir." She reached out to playfully push one hand against his shoulder and he caught her bare fingers in his, trapping her touch and impulsively extending the contact.

He waited for her to hesitate, to demand that he take no such liberties or chide him for coming to her alone. He meant to prove to her that no matter what he'd demonstrated in the gazebo, he was perfectly capable of restraint and gentlemanly conduct.

Capable, yes.

Her youth and inexperience meant she was relying on his self-discipline and stronger will to prevail over hers. But when Raven Wells placed her bare fingers over his heart a thousand trails of fire began to work through his body and her eyes met his without shame —there was nothing to prove.

"Will you ask me to dance on Saturday, Mr. Warrick?"

"You and no other."

"How scandalous!" she gasped with a mischievous gleam in her eyes. "You will set every woman in the county against me, sir!"

He touched her chin to tip her face up toward his. "Would you rather I didn't? Shall I appease them and make a show of filling up dance cards?"

"No."

"I see. So I am to stand against the wall with a foreboding scowl on my face while you take the floor with all those 'local young bucks'?" he teased.

She looked at him through the flirtatious veil of her dark lashes. "Will you?"

"I have decided that when it comes to you, Raven Wells, I will always strive to be first."

"First?"

"You gifted me with your first kiss and I hope with your first dance…" He reached up with his hand to touch the velvet soft curve of her face. "I find that I am hungry to retain the privilege to always be first in all things when it comes to you."

"You and no other hold that privilege, sir," she whispered.

He kissed her. He kissed her because to not kiss her was an impossibility. Only this time, there was no preamble of cautious exploration. The embers of desire ignited at the first touch of his lips to hers and time folded to create the illusion that he had never let her go. Civilized restraint evaporated when she sighed against him, melting into his frame so that the weight and contours of her body were pressed toward his. Her mouth parted for the onslaught of his tongue, an eager offering that proved his beautiful siren had forgotten none of the lessons of the gazebo.

Wildfire swept through his veins, so fast that he knew he had to slow them down. He lifted his chin to deny her access to his mouth but Raven's hunger was not so easily thwarted. She shyly kissed his throat instead, her tongue flicking shyly over his adam's apple and making him groan. His arms tightened around her, lifting her from the floor.

"Am I hurting you?" she asked softly.

"Not at all," Phillip shook his head with a smile. "Here, allow me to demonstrate."

"Wha-what?"

He turned the tables on her, sliding his mouth down the pulse of her neck. Raven's reaction was clear. He'd meant to teach her a lesson on just how delectable her touch had felt but as she arched her back, writhing against him, sighing and gasping, Phillip was lost.

"Yes!" She cried out sweetly. "Oh, my! This is....impossible! Phillip!"

Her innocent candor was beyond disarming. Other women may have pretended a weak protest while their hands were finding the buttons to his pants but there was no mistaking the genuine surprise and fearless fire in Raven's eyes. It was power he had never known to show her what a kiss could bring—and a paralyzing responsibility.

"Please don't stop!" she pleaded tipping her head to one side to offer the enticing porcelain of her neck to taste. "It's so lovely!"

Oh, god. My beautiful shameless girl!

He complied to gently kiss the warm column of her neck again, lingering briefly at the well behind her ear only to land at the juncture where her shoulder sloped across, playfully grazing the most sensitive points of her skin with his teeth.

Raven clung to him, shuddering and dancing on the tips of her toes to stretch upward, as a flower following the sun. His hands sought her skin, exploring only what he could reach. Modest fashions gave him very little but Phillip was in no mood to complain. Even so, it was too easy to lightly trail over fabric and imagine the flesh beneath, the contours and textures of her breasts; Phillip covered the rise of her breasts, cupping them to take full measure of the bounty that was Raven.

"More, oh, please, whatever this is I beg you not to stop!"

Damn it! He lifted her up against him, kissing her again to sample the hot silk of her mouth, the velvet of her tongue; pressing her against his frame, willing her to become aware of just how much he needed her. Raven transformed into a sensual human vine entwining her fingers into his hair and ranging over his back and shoulders, eagerly seeking to map his body.

"Yes, oh, yes!"

"What is the meaning of this?" Trent's voice was as startling to the pair as a gunshot and Phillip released her immediately to put her on her feet before shifting to shield her with his back while Raven quickly readjusted her skirts and tried to restore her hairpins. Phillip winced at the humiliating awareness that the buttons of his pants were straining to hold his raging erection and if Trent hadn't come in, it would be hard to deny where things were headed.

I can lie to myself if I wish but those silk pillows on the floor would have served and...shit!

Of all the ways he'd wanted to present his attachment to Miss Wells to Trent, being discovered in a completely inappropriate embrace in the man's solarium was very near the bottom. "I apologize, Lord Trent." Phillip kept his voice steady. "It is entirely my fault. Miss Wells has done nothing to encourage my—"

"Raven, to your room. Leave, Mr. Warrick and I alone to talk."

Her sigh of defeat was quiet enough that only Phillip could hear it, but she obediently stepped out with her head held high. "Your lord-ship. Please."

"Go." Trent's voice was as yielding as granite and Raven was forced to leave without a word, no doubt convinced that whatever she said would only make things worse for Phillip.

Damn. If he throws me out, I'm going to have to kidnap that woman.

Hell, when did my life become a penny novel?

"Warrick." Geoffrey came closer and eyed him the way a general would an errant officer. "I know you're expecting a bit of a tantrum but we are grown men and too seasoned for the scene, don't you think?"

"Too seasoned?"

"Can I say that you are still young, Warrick, a man in his prime at twenty-eight without admitting to being the dusty old man?"

"You're hardly old, Lord Trent, and I would hope to be old enough not to use youth as an excuse for my behavior." Phillip squared his shoulders. "I'm not a child to cry ignorance."

Trent smiled. "It's to your credit then. But Raven..." His smile faded. "She is not for you."

It was the last thing he'd expected to hear and shock tempered his reply. "Pardon me? Does that mean that you have another suitor in mind?"

"No. In truth, no," Geoffrey shook his head. "Not exactly, but the Phillip Warrick I have come to know, the one who decries gambling and has fiercely guarded his conduct since I met him last—earning a reputation for his serious attention to his duties..." Geoffrey sighed. "You need a woman made of sterner stuff, with an eye to economy and a simpler spirit."

"I'd die of boredom."

"That's what you think but trust me. Slow and steady wins the race." The earl's tone took on a fatherly note. "It's my turn to apologize for spoiling Raven so. She'll make an ambitious match in London this season thanks to word of her vast dowry. She will plague some filthy rich man with her philosophies and pretty looks. But you're a sensible soul, my boy. All the wealth in England should not induce you to marry against your better judgment."

Phillip had to close his eyes for a moment against the torrent of disbelief coursing through him. He opened them with a determination to clarify his position. "I am apparently less sensible than you believe and do not aspire to all the wealth in England."

Trent held up a hand to stop him. "There is no harm in a kiss if that is the extent of it—is that the extent of it so far, Warrick?"

"Yes, but that hardly—"

"Then all is well." Geoffrey straightened his coat. "I will naturally address Raven about her unladylike display and remind her that my generosity and substantial provisions for her future will not stand for another lapse in her judgment. As for you, Mr. Warrick, I know that you will refrain from all unseemly contact with my ward during your stay."

"Raven is innocent, Lord Trent! There is no need to reprimand her since I had every intention of approaching you to—"

"Mr. Warrick. Slow and steady wins the race."

Phillip's jaw dropped and before he could compose a response to the earl's cryptic words, the man turned on his heels and left Phillip standing alone in the storm of his thoughts. "What the hell was that?"

Did he mean to say that I should persist in my courtship but at a more respectful pace? Did he mean to forbid me? "She is not for you" does not exactly fit with "there is no harm in a kiss"!

Phillip made his way to an oversized chair by a potted palm and sat down as his legs numbed. *I should at least celebrate that I'm not packing my bags but I'll be damned if I know what I'm supposed to do next...*

One thing was clear.

Until her guardian physically threw him from the house, he wasn't going to give up an inch of ground. The mention of that "ambitious match" had carved his plans into stone and he'd be damned if he would lose her to another man without a fight.

* * *

THE KNOCK on her door was firm but not too frightening. "Come in."

Geoffrey entered and then closed the door behind him. "Where is your maid?"

"Downstairs."

"Good. Then we can speak with some assurance of privacy." He took another three steps in the room and stopped, suddenly staring around him. "Odd! I've never been in this room, have I? It is not unpleasant, is it?"

Raven blinked a few times, familiar with her guardian's propensity for diversion. "It is a lovely bedroom and I can't recall a reason that would have brought you over its threshold until now." She took a deep breath to let it out slowly. "I am mortified of what you must think of me—of Mr. Warrick—of us!"

"Pphht!" He waved her words away. "Who am I to judge these things?"

"What?" She kept her distance. "You...are my guardian and I assumed that judgment in these things would be precisely what your duties would include."

"Yes, of course." He sighed. "As you wish. Then I must tell you that London is full of men with greater wealth, loftier titles and estates that make Oakwell Manor look like a tradesman's shack."

"I don't care."

"Raven," he said with a smile. "I know I asked you to be kind to Mr. Warrick but I certainly hope you haven't felt compelled to snog the man on my behalf!"

She gasped in outrage at the suggestion. "I have done nothing on your behalf! What a terrible thing to say!"

"Not all that terrible, my dear. Snogging is not an unenjoyable task. But here, let me be clear. I have given Phillip fair warning that you have wonderful prospects awaiting you this Season and that he would be wiser to choose a dull woman who thinks embroidery the pinnacle of feminine achievements."

Raven pressed her lips into a thin line to keep from answering too quickly. "I am grateful, Lord Trent, for the hopes you harbor for me this Season but I truly believe that no greater happiness awaits me. Mr. Warrick is all I want in this world."

"Perhaps." Geoffrey crossed his arms. "But indulge me, Raven. Let us test his resolve, shall we? After all, if your man is cut from truly honorable cloth, then he will pursue you despite my hints that if he takes you from this house, then that is all he will take from me."

"I don't understand."

"I fear he desires you only for whatever dowry you possess, Raven."

"Oh!" Her throat closed at the unexpected idea, fear gripping her. "Did he…say as much?"

"No. But you'll never know for certain if you start bleating otherwise! Say nothing of money to him. Ever." Geoffrey's gaze narrowed. "I cannot forbid you to do as you want. I am old enough to know that doing so is the quickest way to ruin. However I want you to hear what I am saying, girl."

She nodded, waiting like an accused prisoner for her sentence.

"When it comes to love, there is no direct path. Stand your ground. If Mr. Warrick is the man you want, then all should fall into place. If he desires you without mention of your dowry, then when the moment comes, you'll know what to do. Trust your instincts. However, if Phillip starts questioning you about your allowance, you'll know the true cause and you will have your first lesson in just what a fortune hunter looks like." He shrugged his shoulders as if either choice were equally weighted. "All the better to arm yourself for Town, don't you think?"

Phillip has never mentioned money to me! I think that there is nothing in our way and I shall tell him as much!

"Thank you, Lord Trent!" She rushed forward to embrace him. "You are the soul of generosity and I don't know how I will ever thank you for this chance!"

He kept his arms stiffly at his side, awkwardly submitting to her emotional display. "Raven! You are crushing my cravat."

She shyly freed him, regretting the impulse when such gestures tended to darken her guardian's mood. But this time, he only smiled.

"You never disappoint, duchess."

She had to grip her hands behind her back to keep from seizing him again. He was the closest thing she had to family, his approval a fleeting and elusive prize. "I never want to."

CHAPTER 10

*P*hillip left the house, stalking out to find a path that led toward a small decorative lake on the property, created no doubt by some designer decades before to provide a great vantage point of the estate. Like every structure and area of Oakwell Manor, nothing seemed unplanned or without purpose.

The solarium had sealed his heart's fate. What had him flummoxed was that the next natural step eluded him. Nothing in his experience had prepared him for the strange turns of the Earl of Trent waving him off with odd speeches about time to be had and the advantages of boring women. He'd been ready to ask for Raven's hand then and there before Geoffrey had urged him to choose a better time.

He's testing me. Instead of demanding I marry her, he's dangling about and giving me advice on courtship. But why?

How do I not measure up?

His position was secure enough, his fortunes on the rise; certainly he had money enough to afford a wife and Raven would be Lady Warrick, her children provided an inheritance and legacy any woman would be proud to claim. So where was the hindrance?

"Slow and steady wins the race." Phillip repeated the words and stood to look back across to the manor house. "God, why does that sound so hard?"

The answer to his question came racing up the gravel path with a smile, her gait as easy and carefree as a colt's. "I was hoping to catch you, sir."

"Raven." Phillip took a deep breath to steady himself, determined to say his piece before her touch unraveled him. "We cannot keep meeting alone like this, but we must talk."

She slowed, some of her joy muted. "Oh. As you wish."

"Lord Trent is…" he began and then decided that this conversation required a more comfortable distance between them and any watchful eyes in the house. "Here, come." He took her hand and spotted a makeshift haven for their retreat. He drew her toward a large log that was set into the shade of several willow trees. The ground was covered with thick moss and a canopy of hanging willow leaves punctured with sunlight that dappled the place with fleeting laces of light added to a fairy-like aura. They were completely cut off from view from the manor and the path around the lake. He sat her down and then knelt in front of her, keeping both of her hands cradled like wild birds inside the gentle cage of his fingers. "Raven, of all the ways I might have wished to approach your guardian…"

She smiled. "It was horrible, wasn't it?"

"Then why are you grinning?"

She laughed. "Because I'm relieved that it is the means by which we were discovered that troubles you and not some fault with my kisses."

"I have no complaints with your kisses outside of their addictive nature. They must cease and I must cease seeking them or we are both ruined." He forced himself to release her hands and shifted to sit next to her. "I need to prove to Lord Trent that I am not a villain and not the kind of man to take advantage of one so young."

Her brow furrowed. "I am not *so* young."

"You are three weeks away from eighteen and not yet out in society, Miss Wells."

Eyebrows lifted to betray her skepticism. "And by comparison this makes you at ten years my senior, what exactly? A jaded Methuselah?"

"I have experience enough to understand that if I mean to win you, I cannot allow my passion to overrule my sensibilities. The earl made it clear he doesn't think I have the discipline or character to see things through or to adhere to a slower and honorable pace."

"He said that?" she asked.

"He may have but," Phillip said. "I won't give you up, Raven"

"Then don't."

"Nothing is that simple."

Raven sighed. "What are your intentions, Phillip Warrick? Are you going to seduce me and…spoil me….only to throw me aside? Am I to be one of those foolish girls in those novels who is lost to passion?"

"Lost to passion?" He shook his head. "Who talks like that?"

"Is that your answer?" she began to pout and a ricochet of heat blazed through him.

"No. My answer is no. You are not going to one of those foolish girls because my intention is to marry you. I want to ask Trent for your hand in marriage. How does that sound?"

"Like heaven," she said softly. "Except…"

"Yes?" Phillip smiled. "Did I omit something?"

"If your intentions are honorable, can you not seduce me along the way? I mean, does one choice necessarily forbid the other?" She gave him a shy hopeful look. "I have nothing to fear of you, Sir Warrick."

His breath caught in his throat, his spine stiffening as he stood to step back from her. "Damn it. You can't look at me like that and—we're not children playing a game of dare, Raven."

Raven blinked. It was her turn to catch her breath and accept that she was in fact, pushing him very hard. Driving him toward giving her what she desired, even if she wasn't sure where the aching need for him would take her. "No, not a game." She stood to face him, standing close enough to hold him captive as he looked up at her. "Oh, Methuselah, I need your guidance."

"Raven."

"I am caught in a riddle, O' Ancient One. My guardian has not forbidden me to fall in love, sir. And if he had, what attention would I pay? Trent is my guardian and I owe him all obedience but after kissing you in the gazebo, I am somewhat off my tether, sir. It is as if you alone are the voice I would hear or heed. Can you imagine such a thing?"

"Raven." He said her name again, but instead of a reproach his tone conveyed an ache and longing that matched hers.

"Furthermore, Great Sage of Experience, I do not think I will be able to agree to any plan that forbids kissing. I find that I want you to kiss me again very much."

"The risk..."

"I am an optimist and a dreamer, Mr. Warrick." She reached out a hand to rearrange a curl from his cheek, her breath quickening at the phantom tingle of raw power at the move. She was standing between his thighs, above him and something uncoiled inside of her at the sweet supplication in his eyes. "Nothing in the glittering fantasy of London holds a candle to you, Mr. Warrick."

He shook his head. "You mustn't..."

She smiled and slowly began to lean down until her lips hovered a scant inch above his. "It is Spring and I care nothing for the Fall. Kiss me, Phillip."

It was a woman's logic and he was an enrapt captive.

If I intend to marry her, with or without Trent's permission—is it really so wrong? If an honorable end is assured, what matters the path...

It was a cad's logic, a rogue and a rake's reasoning but as her breath fanned out to tease and torment his lips, so close it was as if he could already taste her kisses, Phillip no longer cared. He had found her. The woman of his dreams: clever beyond reckoning, a creature of light and laughter, Raven was pure joy and in his arms, his angel became a shameless siren that trembled in his arms.

It is Spring and I care nothing for the Fall.

She kissed him, melting into him in a slow, glorious cascade of sensation.

Raven savored it, the slow surge as her confidence grew, for Phillip yielded control to her, guiding her only by responding to her touch and demonstrating his pleasure. Power added a dimension to her desire, to the potency of it. She loved the sensation that he was struggling to maintain a line in the sand; that the pleasure she inflicted could sweep him into her arms.

In the solarium, she'd reveled in the firm lines of his body, marveling at the heat of his frame through his coat and shirt. But now, in this private glade and with caution lost to the winds, she wanted more. A restless, anxious frustration nibbled at her, a hot unfamiliar tension begging her to solve the mystery of a mechanism that screamed for release.

Raven unbuttoned his shirt and dispensed with the layers that kept him from her. Coarse silken curls a dark tawny brown that echoed his coloring made for a delightful discovery. It was a light mat across his frame with a wicked trail of hair that disappeared into his pants. She gasped at the sight of his chest—a muscled wall that was so firm and at the same time, his skin was velvet under that dusting of hair. She leaned in to kiss him again, wrapping her legs around him to settle in to the business of pushing his coat and shirt from his shoulders.

For a second or two, he was helpless with his arms tangled in the cloth and he moaned in frustration. For she alone could touch him, while he was her willing prisoner. It was too tempting a conundrum for Raven to waste.

"Raven."

"Shh. Be very still. I am learning you."

If kissing Phillip's throat was even a pale echo of the effect of his mouth against her neck, several new theories came to life that demanded exploration. She shyly began on the familiar lines of his throat, this time deliberately trying to evoke his groans. His skin smelled faintly of cinnamon and sandalwood, and she reveled in the taste of him. Raven was able to determine that a playful combination of her tongue and her teeth was best. As if pain and pleasure were somehow one and the same for a man...

She kissed his collar bone and lightly raked his upper shoulders with her fingernails. Then boldly moved downward to kiss one of the tight peaks so like her own. She knew how sensitive her breasts were and within the space of heartbeat as she latched onto his coral ruddy skin, she knew his body was the masculine echo to hers.

"Raven! Get this coat off me!"

She leaned back, mischief and fire warring in her eyes. After all, freeing him meant yielding her newfound power but it also freed Phillip to touch her as she desperately needed him to.

"Will you behave if I free you?"

He shook his head. "Not a chance of it, Raven Wells."

"Thank god!" Raven pushed the bulk of the cloth downward, past his elbows, and he was able to pull his arms free.

Phillip smiled. He was so far past a useless grab at good behavior it was comical.

He dropped his coat and shirt on the mossy ground as an improvised blanket beneath them, and lowered her onto it. The buttons of her bodice yielded to his touch and he kissed every inch he bared until Raven's hands were just as eager to aid him in his quest. She giggled as the barriers fell, sighing with relief as he dispensed with her corset with an efficient maneuver that popped the front fastenings without wasting time on the back laces.

Within seconds, the bounty that was Raven Wells was laid out for him. Naked to the waist, her breasts were firm and high, as ample as autumn apples, twin orbs with dark pink tips jutting out to the sky. She was soft curves and gentle lines, her skin unmarred, the color of cream. She was slender but not rail-thin or frail and it was impossible not to admire the alluring health of a goddess turned woman. Raven began to cover herself with her hands but when his expression betrayed his disappointment, she stopped and then won him over for all time by stretching her arms over her head with a shy smile.

"It pleases you to look?" she asked softly.

"God, yes," he said lowering himself to take her into his arms. "You are pure sorcery, woman."

He began touching her in a playful dance that aroused but barely teased her skin, his fingertips lightly trailing around the swell of her breasts, the tender underside of each mound, each concentric circle daring to come a tiny bit closer to the small tips, her flesh puckered and tight, dark rose peaks with thick pert nipples that demanded his touch. She arched her back, her eyes fluttering closed and he kissed her and then covered her breasts with his hands, gently pressing the warm wells of his palms across her, a whisper of contact, before he lowered his head to suckle first one and then the other.

She was bucking and writhing beneath him, her hands restlessly stroking and clawing at his back and shoulders. And everything began to accelerate in a sizzling race to satisfy themselves.

He captured one of her hands and guided it down to press her palm against his rock hard arousal, the barrier of his pants hiding nothing of the shape and mass of his cock. He stopped kissing her to lift his head, taking in the widening of her eyes, the flutter of her lashes in shock and the slow shift as a new heated possibility came to her.

He did not expect her to push him off but even in the heat of the moment, a portion of his soul demanded that he offer her the chance to retreat.

"I will be bold where others are cautious," she whispered.

"What was that?" Phillip asked, surprised at the phrase on her lips.

"I am not afraid." She lifted up to kiss him and the moment of reversal passed forever.

Her fingers moved of their own accord and Phillip moaned as his world narrowed to the span of her small hands as they worked up and over his taut flesh. The buttons were dispensed with and he shuddered as his cock sprang free to land in her waiting hands.

Tentative strokes from trembling fingers gave way as his arousal stiffened even more, bobbing up as if to seek the hot soft pads of her hands. She covered the swollen tip of him, sending a shiver of sweet fire up his spine. The flow of blood to his cock felt like hot sand trickling through him to pool there, the power of his sex gathering in a delicious storm that she alone summoned.

"It is so...strange and noble, isn't it?" she sighed and he kissed her for it. He kissed her for being so sweet and wild and Raven.

He covered her hand to guide her touch, teaching her what pleased him best and then realized his mistake. For Raven was an apt and eager pupil and when she added the faintest drag of her fingernails to the game, Phillip held his breath and prayed he didn't spend himself.

Too quick. God, when did I ever feel this rush? Boasting...about....how I took every woman at my leisure...who was that fool? My innocent Raven is holding the reins now and I am flying!

It was all happening much more swiftly than he wished but every effort to slow her backfired. There was nothing to be done. Phillip knew he'd forfeited civility—forfeited every layer of restraint, stripped to a primal need to achieve her.

"Raven," he said as he pulled back to part her thighs, to reach up under her skirts and when his fingers encountered folds so slick and so hot it made his breath seize up in his chest. She was already so wet, so ready, it shook him. He'd meant to prepare her, to ensure that her desire would be a match for the impending moment he couldn't delay, but the honey that coated his fingertips ignited a dark storm that roared through him.

Meant to…should…a better man would…

The words lost meaning.

He pushed her skirts up around her waist and positioned his hips between her thighs, the swollen tip of his cock notching up against the silky damp fire of her entrance. He hesitated, his eyes closing as the sweet promise of her body beckoned him—but Raven managed to surprise him once again.

She arched up, her channel seizing him, crying out as he encountered her virginal barrier. Phillip kissed her to ease the pain, distracting her for just a few seconds before he reared back and then took her completely in one masterful and forceful thrust that irrevocably ended the dilemma.

He held only long enough for her channel to accept him, stretching to hold him fast. Phillip kissed her neck again, whispering a stream of soothing promises into the curve of her ears, rewarded as she relaxed and the molten confines of her body beckoned him on.

She didn't shrink from him, from any of it. Her thighs widened and she urged him to move into her, wrapping her legs around his waist and pressing her heels into his lower back. She moaned and writhed beneath him and Phillip fell back into the race. He withdrew and returned, each stroke a revelation for them both.

She was so tight, her muscles gripping and releasing him in a mystery of possession and power. Thrusting, thrusting, faster and faster, until he was sure he was flying, soaring, tethered to the earth only by Raven until the red hot sand pooling between his hips electrified and he knew he was close.

Close and then gone...his world contracted into a spasm of white-searing ecstasy, a release that ripped from him in jetting torrents that robbed him of all language. His climax shuddered and then peaked again, forcing him to cry out.

Phillip sagged against her, struggling to balance on his elbows to keep from crushing her. He was not a novice at the arts of love, but it was all he could do not to weep at the strength of an orgasm that had wrenched him free of his existence.

It took several seconds before he could think clearly enough to speak.

"Raven...that was...not how I....hoped..."

"No?" she asked, her voice filled with concern. "Did I do it wrong?"

He shook his head. "No, but I definitely could have done better by you." His breathing was ragged as he gently kissed her forehead and then the tip of her nose.

"Truly?" she asked breathlessly. "How marvelous!"

He knew she hadn't climaxed but the reality that she had no notion of how selfish the encounter had been was nearly his undoing. "Raven. It will be. I promise."

She sighed and wriggled in contentment, inadvertently forcing Phillip to hold his breath as he was treated to an after-shock from his overly sensitive flesh still held in the grip of her body. A faint echo of a secondary climax unfurled from his spinal cord and Phillip prayed he didn't faint from the delicious torment of it.

"Woman. Don't. Move."

Raven instantly obeyed, but a gleam in her grey eyes told him that he wouldn't always be so lucky. Phillip disengaged as delicately as he could, freeing her from him, wincing at the glimpse of blood on her thighs. "Are you all right?" he asked her cautiously, making an intense study of her face for any hint of hurt or fear.

She smiled at him. "I feel wonderful though a bit strange…"

"Strange?"

"Strange because I do not know myself anymore. I have the urge to sleep in your arms but also to run and dance about like a pagan queen; and cannot decide which impulse would be wise." Raven laughed. "If being deflowered parts me from my reason, I shall have to begin preparing myself for bedlam, Phillip. For I don't think I wish to stop. Ever."

He chuckled and kissed the top of her head then rolled away to tuck himself away and rebutton his pants. "We are already mad. Oh, god, I know I am supposed to start moaning apologies but I am not sorry, Raven. God help me. If regret comes later, it will only be at your bidding." He kissed her forehead, a weak attempt to cool his ardor. "To hell with it, I'll speak to the earl before another hour passes and if it goes badly, we can elope."

"Phillip," she sighed and raised herself up to her knees to kiss his temples and smooth his brow with the cool blades of her fingers. "Yes. I want you to speak to Lord Trent but…I think we must choose the hour more wisely."

"What are you saying?"

"I am saying, my love, that he has rebuffed the subject once today and I know him. If we rush back with another petition, his temper will refuse you even if his common sense dictates acceptance." She sighed. "If he challenged you to move slowly, than I have spoiled things, haven't I?"

"Nothing is spoiled." Phillip said levelly, struggling not to be distracted by the sight of Raven Wells bared to the waist. "Shall we… give him the impression that things are unfolding…at a more natural pace?" He caught the tip of one pert breast in his mouth and suckled her as she arched her back to beg him for more.

"Phillip!"

He forced himself to lift his head. "Raven. Look at me. Can we do this? Can we—look at each other politely across that dinner table and publicly keep a polite distance for a few days?"

She pouted at the loss of his mouth to her flesh but finally nodded. "Yes, but only if you do not deny me when no one is looking." She retrieved his shirt and coat from the ground and held it out to him, the embodiment of an enticing beauty who would have her way. "You promised to do better, Mr. Warrick."

"Raven Wells, I don't think I will ever be able to deny you— anything. But I am a man of my word and I look forward to it."

CHAPTER 11

"*O*h, no! What's this?" Kitty asked the instant she crossed the threshold of her bedroom. "Don't you dare tell me the gathering is off! I just spent the night finishing those alterations!"

Raven threw herself face down onto the bed with a giggle. "It is on, though what do I care?"

"I'll tell you what you care! That's twenty six yards of fabric and my eyes gone blind finishing that dress in time, mistress." Kitty crossed her arms, a woman possessed. "You'll wear it with beaming smiles and the grace of a queen or I'll snatch the hair off your head!"

Raven lifted her face from the pillows, openly enjoying Kitty's fit. "Such violent threats! How surprising to hear them from a girl as mild as yourself, Miss Polk!"

Kitty's fingers flew to cover her own lips in shock. "I—I'm sorry. But if you knew how I've struggled with those flounces..."

"I meant I'm already so deliriously happy, what do I need of dancing?"

"No one *needs* to dance. Don't be ridiculous. If I know anything about young ladies your age, you're going to measure your life in terms of dance cards so don't you be flopping about over there and sighing on—" Kitty stopped herself abruptly, a new look of suspicion in her eyes. "Why are you so happy?"

Raven shimmied off the bed to elude Kitty's study. "I am always happy. You said yourself it was a marvel. I should rest before dinner. The earl is determined that things continue to go well. I want to wear the blue and that opal choker and diamond hair chain."

"Not too much for a dinner at Oakwell?"

Raven shook her head firmly. "Lord Trent has ordered me to shine, Kitty." *And I want Phillip to be dazzled and see that I am not cowering in shame, but that his touch has made me glow.*

PHILLIP MADE an objective inventory of everything on his plate. Then he did it in French, then Latin, and in one last desperate try, attempted it all in alphabetical order. Even so, nothing could match the sight of Raven wearing an evening gown that bared her neck and shoulders, jewels gleaming at her throat and a rope of diamonds threaded through her ebony curls.

Even Lady Baybrook was mollified to shower her with compliments and poor Mr. Sheffield dropped his knife no less than three times.

Miss Raven Wells had come into her own.

And only Phillip knew the true cause of it. He'd held an innocent in his arms and taken liberties that he might never be able to atone for; but regret failed to overtake him. Instead there was only the promise of a future full of passion and true happiness.

It was only a matter of time.

"What a fuss over bunting!" the earl growled. "Apparently no ball is sanctioned without a sufficient amount of bunting!"

"Decorations speak to your level of taste, Lord Trent," Lady Baybrook advised. "Think of it as an opportunity rather than a burden, sir."

Geoffrey laughed darkly. "An opportunity to empty my purse and have my pockets picked!"

"What colors have you chosen?" Lady Morley asked.

"Gold and jade green," he replied. "Not much of a stretch since the ballroom is edged in gilt and the floors are inlaid green marble. Let me be honest, I'm not refurnishing my house! I don't care how many of the county's finest sniff the drapes, there is only so far I am willing to go to accommodate them."

"They will express nothing but gratitude and joy at your generosity, I am sure of it." Raven smiled at him.

"Sure, are you?" Trent shook his head. "My dear girl, you always see the best in everyone and all things. However shall I protect you?" He looked at Phillip. "Like a lamb amidst wolves, eh, Warrick?"

Phillip did his best to summon his best poker face. "Yes but thanks to you, I think that lamb has the intelligence and wit needed to keep far ahead of the pack."

"Right you are! How right you are!" Trent smiled, his mood openly improving. "Woe betide the predator that thinks one flash of teeth will give them victory. What say you, Raven?"

"Gracious! Is it a dance or a gladiatorial arena where I will be chained to a post and facing wild dogs? If so then I shall have to rethink my choice of accessories!" Raven said.

"There, there, my dear. You will conquer London with nothing more dangerous than a fan and a wicked smile, won't you?" Trent reached over to lift his glass in her direction. "A man has no defense against a woman's weaponry."

Raven blushed. "Now I don't know if I'm arming for a debut or a battle."

"Are they not the same thing?" the earl taunted her. "But enough of this. My Raven has no need to concern herself with any of it. A social season of dancing will blur to memory before I need worry about sorting through offers of marriage and the dull business that separates me from my ward. I have no desire to rush toward that day and if any man tries to push me, I'll cut him off at the knees."

"So much for the local bucks enjoying the evening." Mr. Sheffield noted.

Phillip re-inventoried his peas. Raven's wisdom at postponing his petition was obviously reinforced but it didn't make him more comfortable. He'd deflowered the girl and while there would yet be a London season, she would arrive as a married woman and not a debutante—an altogether different proposition. But he made a mental note to be sure to provide her with the loveliest season in London he could to ensure that there was no lacking or question of sacrifice.

"—agree, Mr. Warrick?"

"Pardon?" Phillip realized he'd missed Mr. Carlton's question. "I'm so sorry. I was...lost in thought."

It was not the time to look at Raven but there was no stopping himself. They were lost together and it gave him courage.

Lord Morley tapped his glass to have it refilled. "The man is too polite to admit that he is bored with conversation about bunting and the prospects for Miss Wells' dance cards. God, what man wouldn't be? I've heard of nothing else for days as if my wife's brain had been emptied of all else!"

"I hope I have not overtaxed you with the subject, my dear," Lady Morley said softly. "It has been so long since I've danced!"

"Quiet your prattling, Millicent! You only underline my point and you dance more than any respectable woman has a right to!" Lord Morley rolled his eyes in disgust. "A married woman!"

"Don't be too hard on her, Lord Morley," Trent said. "There's not a female on the grounds who isn't waxing a bit poetic these days. But come, cheer up and tell me that you are looking forward to the shooting tomorrow."

Talk turned to guns and the prospects of the men's outing, and Phillip participated as best as he could. He'd packed two rifles in anticipation of the entertainment and at last, was able to keep up with the banter of the party.

The women withdrew as the meal finished and Phillip breathed a sigh of relief. He'd survived his first foray into overt deception under Trent's discerning nose.

One dinner down. A dozen treacherous tests yet ahead...

Phillip stopped in his room after the women departed to the salon to retrieve the gift of cigars for Trent he'd forgotten to bring with him only to find Mr. Timms holding his shirt aloft to make a study of a green stain across the shoulders.

"Timms."

"I'm sorry, sir. I was just—seeing what I can make of this. Did you have a mishap, Mr. Warrick?"

Hardly, but I suppose that depends on which side of this you land on.

"I was lounging in the grass by the lake and may have...slipped."

Mr. Timms shook his head. "I believe I have something to save it, sir. It is too fine a linen to sacrifice. But the coat, the lining will need replacing."

Phillip nodded. "Do what you can. Thank you, Mr. Timms."

"Did you come up for something, sir?"

"I brought a small box of cigars and wished to offer them to the others." Phillip pulled a wrapped parcel from a drawer next to the bed. "I remembered that Lord Trent had a fondness for rare blends."

"You remember rightly. Though he loathes snuff and will deride any man who uses it in his presence." Mr. Timms stepped back to allow Phillip to take his leave.

"A good bit of knowledge to tuck away." Phillip turned to go then stopped. "Timms?"

"Yes, Sir Warrick?"

"No need to wait up. I think we'll go late and I can see myself to bed."

"Very good, sir." Mr. Timms nodded. "I am very appreciative to the courtesy since I'll be faring better than most of the manservants. Sleep is harder and harder to come by as the ball draws closer. Some of the staff will be up the next two nights through to prepare the house so I shouldn't be surprised if you see a few souls in the halls at every hour."

"Oh, how...difficult for them!" His hopes of slipping into Raven's rooms to make good on his promises faded quickly at the news, but he was relieved to avoid detection. Though the coincidence of Timms' well-timed advice was a little unsettling.

"They'll be waiting for you downstairs, sir."

"Yes. I don't want to—disappoint."

Even if I'm destined to do exactly that...

CHAPTER 12

The following afternoon, rain spoiled the shooting but the earl insisted on the men trekking out to his hunting lodge, undoubtedly to drink and smoke undisturbed. Last night, Trent's dark mood had dominated after dinner and when he'd ordered the men to keep him company into the wee hours, one look from Phillip had conveyed his regrets. The day's male outing was merely an extension of the earl's unexplained possessive temperament. She was used to the mercurial changes in Trent's behavior and only prayed that Phillip would endure and find some humor in his kidnapping.

Raven watched the water trail over the solarium's large windows and took solace in the beauty of it. She had never found rain to be a sorrowful event, and today's downpour was no different. She only wished that Phillip was within reach.

I will tell him that I once danced in the rain and used to believe that my father was the King of Clouds because of the color of my eyes. He'll laugh and then he'll kiss me...

"I received your note of invitation, Miss Wells." Lady Morley appeared in the doorway, holding out the folded paper in question as if proof were required before she could enter the room.

Raven turned with a smile. "I'm so glad! Tea is always very nice on a day like this, but even better when shared."

Millicent nodded and walked in to admire the space. "A lovely setting for it, though unconventional."

"Only unconventional if I insisted we use the floor cushions! But here," she gestured toward the softest chair. "Let's pretend we are marooned on a tropical island and worlds away from worry about what is proper."

"I would like that!" Lady Morley sat down, arranging her skirts as Raven brought out the tea trolley and set the tray on the low table between them.

"What woman in corsets wouldn't?"

Millicent smiled. "You do have a refreshing wit, Miss Wells."

"Thank you. Some are not so charmed by my humor."

"Some, like my husband," Lady Morley said softly. "I have convinced him that I share his opinion of you, Miss Wells. I hope you'll forgive me for the vicious lies I have given voice beyond your hearing."

Raven smiled. "I'm only relieved he believes them."

"My husband is…" Lady Morley took up her tea cup, her hands shaking. "You must put what you've seen from your mind. These matters are beyond you, Miss Wells. I know you mean well, but you have yourself to see to, Miss Wells. Do not trouble with my…situation. You are too young to be bothered with the—"

"Age is not an impediment to concern, Lady Morley, and I think you are too young to consign yourself to despair." Raven set her cup down. "I have spent sleepless nights and most of my days thinking of you and your situation as you put it."

"It is not your business to be so occupied!" Millicent said frostily as she began to withdraw, clearly preparing to leave.

Raven reached out and caught the woman's hand. "You're right. It is none of my business, your ladyship. I am young and easily dismissed. But I want to help you. If there is aid to be rendered, you may be surprised to discover that I am an extremely formidable person."

Millicent held her place and did not pull her hand away from Raven's gentle grip. "How is that possible? What does a girl like you know of...the world?"

"I am forbidden to speak of this. But as you have been forced to trust me with your secrets, it is only fair to give you mine. I do not know my parents. I was placed in the care of a vicar and his wife when I was a very small infant. They were childless and happy to take me in. I was a spoiled and carefree thing, Lady Morley." Raven swallowed the lump in her throat, determined to make a strong showing. "I was cherished and still think of them as my true family. The reverend would read to me and let me rest my head against his shoulder while I fell asleep. And she was—"

Raven covered her lips and waited for the pain to subside. She'd been years under their roof and tender care. A thousand memories washed over her of ghostly kisses and laughter. "I was nine when they died from a cholera outbreak."

"Oh, my! How horrible!"

"I was an orphan in every sense of the word. No one stepped forward to take me and without legitimate family, I was sent to a public house for unwanted children. It was a cold miserable hole, Lady Morley. The proprietors believed that our only salvation lay in hunger, hard work and beatings. The woman who had our keeping said we were vile animals and products of sin and—"

"Say no more! I cannot bear it!"

Raven relented. "I was there for two years before the earl visited on some charitable call and found me. He was inspired to take me under his wing and I have thanked Providence every day for it."

"It's like a novel!"

"A very unbelievable novel," Raven amended with a smile. "So you see, I may be young but I have walked more roads than most and I know what it is to be in a bad place and to desire nothing more than escape."

"What could you possibly do to help?" she whispered.

"Tell me what you would want."

Millicent shook her head. "There is no hope. It would be too much to—"

"Tell me what you pray for, Lady Morley."

"I want to get away from him." It was barely a whisper, but the power of uttering the words aloud brought tears to both their eyes.

Raven nodded. "We will see to it together."

"My god."

"Before the holiday ends, I swear it." Raven let out a long slow breath to steady her nerves. "Perhaps I can ask Mr. Warrick to assist me in—"

"No! No one else can know of my intentions! Especially not a man who will feel honor bound to alert my husband!"

"Phillip is too kind to betray you, I am sure of it!"

Lady Morley shook her head, her eyes reflecting a bitter wisdom beyond her years. "Even if it broke his heart to do so, he would fall in line with the law and with his loyalties to his sex. Please, Miss Wells. You must tell no one of what we contemplate. Swear it."

Raven nodded. "I swear that I shall not breathe a word to any other living soul of our aims. Though, I must confess my maid is already a co-consipirator."

"The salve that Mrs. Lindstrom procured?"

"Just so. Kitty is a dear and has already held your secret close to her heart."

Lady Morley sighed. "As is my maid, but it can go no further!"

"Our club will not grow in membership, not female and certainly not in male membership unless I have your consent. You have my solemn vow. And now let us come up with a plan."

There was nothing to do but pour more tea, and with their heads bent together, quietly hatch a plot worthy of a gothic penny novel and cling to the hope that happiness was indeed every woman's right.

CHAPTER 13

*I*t was an act of pure daring that brought her to his door when the house was asleep but Raven was determined. The men had missed dinner after their soggy exile in the hunting lodge and Kitty had told her that the earl had gotten so foxed that Mr. Sheffield and Mr. Warrick had carried him up the steps into the house. She suspected that Phillip's day had been a damp, miserable excursion but she was too impatient to see him again to wait another night. Her afternoon with Lady Morley had shaken her spirits and she needed to hear his voice and feel safe.

"Phillip, it's me. I'm sorry to push in but it was such a long day without you—" She'd spoken as she came into his room but the sight of him without a nightshirt sitting in the midst of his bed was an end to speech. Gleaming shafts of moonlight cut across the room and a single lit taper was all that remained of his evening's rituals before sleep.

"Raven! Timms said there are servants preparing for the ball working late in the halls. I'm not sure this is such a good idea."

"It's mostly completed on the ground floor and I'm not foolish enough to insist on carrying a taper about to draw attention to myself!" She crossed her arms impatiently. "This is not the joyous greeting I was hoping for, Phillip."

He smiled. "Joyous? I'm so relieved to see you I feel like crying. How's that for joy?"

"Better." She put her hands on her hips. "Now say something sweet and flattering, Warrick, please."

"I have never seen you with your hair down before, Raven."

Her brow furrowed. "Was that praise?"

"I can't think when I look at you. Damn it, woman. You are incomparable and you know it! I am not the kind of man to recite poetry about the silk of your hair but my heart aches staring at you and I should warn you that unless your ultimate aim for this intrusion is me bedding you until you are senseless, you need to turn around this instant, Miss Wells."

"That was very sweetly said," she smiled at him. "I confess, my plan was not very thorough. I just...was feeling restless and...it was a bit uncomfortable at first when we...but you led me to believe the experience improves, which seems unlikely if you ask me...so...I wanted..."

He smiled back at her as his grip tightened on his bedding in frustration. "It's been a long night *and* a long day, Raven! But I am rethinking the safety of our agreement in the glade after spending a day trapped in a lodge listening to that man rant while cleaning his guns. If he finds you here, he'll kill me." Phillip ran both hands through his hair. "But not touching you..."

She latched the door quietly and stood with her back against it. "It is a tangle, isn't it?" She sighed, then asked softly, "Do you really think he'll kill you?" Alarm seized her and she pressed a hand against her racing heartbeat. "I didn't consider that. I'm so sorry."

"Raven, no apologies. Remember?" He held out his hand. "Come to bed, woman."

"Well, not if it means your death, Phillip," she countered, a hint of mischief in her eyes. "Though I give us great praise for our indifferent performance last night at dinner, don't you?"

"I misspoke. A bomb could go off and I doubt that Lord Trent is in any shape to stir. Who knew I tended toward the dramatic?" He kept his hand outstretched, the invitation open. "Though it occurs to me that I might die if you *don't* get in this bed."

"Oh, well then it is an act of pure mercy! You must not expire on my account, sir." She smiled and rushed toward the sanctuary of his arms.

"Come! You are overdressed to be ravished."

Raven's feet stuttered to a halt just as she reached the bed.

Phillip held his breath. "Raven Wells. No games."

"No games," she whispered. She slowly reached up and began to untie the ribbons of her bodice, drawing out each one and letting it fall from her fingers only when the cut tip slipped past her touch. Her movements were unrelenting, an unpracticed dance of seduction that held him captive. His body twitched at every flick of her wrist and when her gown parted to reveal the firm curves of her breasts, the shadow between them accenting the pert taut points and smooth flesh carved out for his pleasure.

She slipped the dressing gown back from her shoulders and he marveled at the way her waist nipped in flaring out to hips created for his hands. The triangular nest of ebony curls covering her sex beckoned his touch and Raven shamelessly dropped her nightclothes to the floor, stepping out of them as easily as a woman stepping over a mud puddle.

"Oh, my god..." he whispered, a man utterly conquered.

"I want very much to be ravished, Phillip. I want nothing between us."

He didn't need to be asked twice. In one swift move, he shifted forward to catch her arms and pull her up onto the bedding, pinning her beneath him with a possessive growl. Need dictated every move he made but he would savor her in a leisurely game to teach her just how marvelous the act could be.

Selfish, I am not, my lady love!

She had asked him to ravish her but Phillip approached her body with the reverence of an initiate before a pagan altar. She was a study in contrasts.

Kissing her. Shifting them up onto their knees, facing each other.

Raven eagerly reached for him, gripping and stroking him, encircling his flesh with her fingers to encourage pure fire to coil inside of him.

Phillip shook his head, wary of yielding control to her again and failing to hold back. He lifted her from him and shifted her to turn around, moving behind her to change the dynamic. He tipped her head to one side to allow him access to her neck and shoulders, drawing her up against him completely. The position limited her reach but gave him ample freedom. His cock was rock hard nested against the ripe curves of her bottom and his hands swept across her skin and up her rib cage to cup her breasts. He gently squeezed and lifted them, teasing her with the dance of his hands before pinching the aroused tips.

Raven's hips shimmied back against him, a silent plea for him to take her, but Phillip was far from finished. One hand cupped a breast and kept up the sweet game, caressing her and pulling his thumb over the hardened peak, while the other hand slid down slowly, over the soft rise of her belly to move through the rough silken curls covering her venus mons.

Her curls were already wet and Phillip's long fingers found their prize, as Raven instinctively spread her knees to give him what he wanted. His fingers dipped down into the honey-slick folds to find the hard little pearl of her clit and its sensitive root under the velvet of her skin and Phillip began to kiss and tease her neck to echo the dance of his hand over her clit.

Faster and faster, he worked her slick pearl, abandoning it for a few strokes to push her further before sliding back and forth over her most sensitive part until she was nearly mindless with it. Raven rocked against his hand, her head pressing into his shoulder and when he felt her hips start to shudder he knew she was nearly there.

He stopped instantly to keep her from it, and pushed her down onto the bed, rolling her over onto her back to spread out beneath him. She was nearly mindless with her need and Raven held nothing back, her trust was total. Everything he was doing was adding to the haze, transporting her beyond her senses.

He parted her thighs but instead of bringing his cock into the fray,

Phillip smiled at the notion that his lady love was not the only one capable of a good surprise. He knelt between her calves and leaned over to kiss her glistening sex. She lifted up on her elbows, startled enough to start to protest but then she was bucking her hips up to give him more, begging him not to stop.

He held her in place with his palms splayed against her hipbones, pinning her in place as his tongue danced mercilessly against her. It was the most intimate of torments and it humbled him to realize that never before had he been this intoxicated on the sweet taste of a woman. He sensed that she was close and slowed down, lightening the contact until she was crying out for it. His hand stole up to softly muffle her sounds and she clung to his fingers only to push them back toward her breasts.

It was his turn to savor his power over her.

Phillip renewed the rhythm like a man possessed, increasing the pressure of his mouth and moaning against the sweet salt of her excitement until she came in a glorious writhing spasm that he could taste on his lips.

"Phillip!"

"Shh!" He chuckled and added his hand to the game, touching her in a concert of soft strokes and licks that drew out her pleasure. She pressed her own fingers against her lips and Phillip's lust flared to demand its due.

He raised up on his hands and knees and climbed up to cover her with his body, moving until the unmistakable proof of his intentions was notched against the soft wet entrance. There was no need for more of a preamble. Her thighs were already spread wide to welcome him and her arms wrapped around him to celebrate his arrival. At the promise of his first thrust, Raven began to shudder again and Phillip seized the advantage.

He drove into her hard, sheathed to the hilt in the space of a heartbeat. She was so tight but so eager, there was nothing left to hold him in check; everything to spur him on. He pistoned inside of her, thrusting upward in a race to join her in a satisfied finish. She was an endless well of desire and when she began to climax again, Phillip accepted that he could not linger long behind her.

He covered her mouth with his kisses, willing her to taste herself on his lips and the wickedness of the impulse pushed him over the edge. Her tongue lapped at his and Phillip came in a climax that gripped his entire frame as he spent himself inside of her in what seemed like an endless implosion of ecstasy.

He cradled her against his chest, his eyes shut tight while he waited for his soul to reattach to his body. *Holy...gods...*

"Oh, my!" she exclaimed softly. "That was...marvelous!"

He smiled into the pillows, awash in the delicious thrill of being a man proven right. "Was it, my love?"

She playfully struck him on the shoulder. "You know it was! I had no idea that...that was even *possible!*"

He shifted to free her but made sure that she was tucked against his side, his arms still around her. "Only with me," he lied smoothly, aware that she couldn't currently see his face. "Only with your one true love."

"Oh!" she said breathlessly. "How perfect!"

Phillip smiled up at the ceiling. "Yes."

It is perfect.

CHAPTER 14

$\mathcal{T}$he line of carriages pulling up to Oakwell Manor was a sight to behold as footmen with torches ran alongside them in the dark and each glittering party stepped out to add to the pageantry of the night. The county's best families had gathered for the event to show off their status, reconnect with old friends and form new alliances. It was a romantic tradition that demanded attention and in all the pageantry it was impossible not to feel the importance of the moment.

Oakwell blazed with candlelight from every window and the spirit of the house was a tangible thing, as if the manor was pleased to be on display and wished to outshine the party-goers. Despite the fuss over bunting, no detail had been overlooked and the ball room was a shimmering gold and green confection that invited revelry.

Raven waited nervously in her room, allowing Kitty to repair one of the flounces after a thread had given way. "I am late."

"Pssht! The party is steps away and you are not late. Besides, everyone knows it is better to arrive after the first awkward rush."

"Why?" Raven asked. "Why is it better?"

Kitty sat back on her heels, looking up at Raven. "How can anyone as beautiful as you not know the answer to that question?"

Raven crossed her arms. "That makes no sense, Kitty. Tell me why."

"Because you can't stop an empty room, you can't steal its breath or seize your triumph from shadows. Only a crowded room full of guests can fall at your feet, applaud your beauty and ensure that you are never forgotten." Kitty stood. "Makes sense now?"

"Oh." Raven swallowed a show of modest arguments to the contrary. She wasn't sure about triumphs but she was vain enough to acknowledge that Kitty had made some very valid points. "Fashionably late is right on time."

"Good girl." Kitty stepped back to survey her handiwork. "Done and done."

Raven pivoted to inspect her reflection in the mirror and smiled. The purple silk she'd acquired the day of Phillip's arrival had been transformed into the dress of her dreams. The eggplant dark color was woven with an undertone of gold that defied description. Her curves were set off by the daring cut of the bodice though it was not nearly as scandalous as some of the fashions of the day. Her age required a nod to modesty. Although her age also generally required adhering to pastel hues, Raven clung to the jewel tones that flattered her coloring.

She touched her lower lip with her tongue moistening the sensitive flesh and evoking the memory of Phillip's kisses. The encounter by the lake had been a shy preamble to the passion they'd shared last night. She leaned forward to study her face more closely, straining to see if the change were visible.

"What are you thinking over there?" Kitty asked.

"I'm thinking that I need a touch of stain for my lips and cheeks."

"A whisper of a touch," Kitty agreed. "No need to spoil the picture with garish spots on your cheeks."

A whisper of color and a dusting of powder on her skin and Raven decided that there was nothing left to delay the moment. If triumph awaited, she was not sorry of it, but it was Phillip Warrick alone she wished to blind with her beauty.

Well, not blind altogether but I shouldn't mind if after tonight, every woman in England looks like a blank sheep in comparison...

It was a wicked aim but it made her smile, a secretive and mischievous thing.

Raven was ready.

* * *

IT WAS A LARGER affair than Phillip had expected and the house's ground floor overflowed with guests bedecked in their finest. The cool spring night air made it tolerable as every door and window was opened to keep things from turning too warm, especially after the music began and exertions could send weaker souls to seek out fainting couches.

One of the reason Phillip dreaded dances was the crush and airless perfumed humidity of some of London's narrow salons. Why anyone enjoyed the din of a hundred conversations over music was a mystery to him. He looked out across the milling room that shifted to give the dancers room as the musicians tuned to herald the first reel, searching for any sign of Raven. He'd waited at the bottom of the stairs for as long as he could without drawing attention and only prayed he hadn't missed his chance to secure her first dance.

"Are you not jumping into the fray, Mr. Warrick?" Lord Trent asked at his elbow.

"Ah, not just yet." Phillip kept his hands politely clasped behind his back. "I'm surveying the battlefield first."

"Wise boy," Trent nodded. "Though you'd best make your move soon. I've had no less than three very keen mothers inquire as to your marital status and financial disposition."

"God."

"Yes, and because I am a wicked friend, I may have hinted that you were genuinely looking for the next Countess Warrick."

"You did not, sir!" Phillip was aghast at the prospect. "I'll be dodging milk toast all night!"

"Let us hope so," Trent said sagely, a wry grin lighting up his features. "Let us hope so." Trent strolled away, openly pleased with his mischief and the scowl on Phillip's face.

So much for hiding in these ferns!

Phillip stepped out but only to go back out into the main hall, overtly removing himself from the line of fire. Since most of the guests had already arrived and the receiving line was finished, it was a good place to catch his breath. But it also allowed for another view of the manor's grand staircase if Raven ever—

Dear Mother of Heaven...how did I ever think to take this in stride?

His lover and the ruler of his heart was perched at the top of the staircase in the most regal and striking shade of purple he had ever seen. Only when her eyes found him, did she smile and begin her descent. Her gaze never wavered from him and Phillip had to grip the ornately carved ballistrade to stop himself from rushing toward her.

A small diamond tiara in her hair and a wide collar of stones at her throat only completed the illusion of a conquering princess alighting to bless her lowly captain of the guards. She held out a gloved hand, the soft kid leather dyed to compliment her dress, and allowed him to kiss her fingers in greeting. "Mr. Warrick! Did I keep you waiting long?"

He shook his head. *Hell, I'd have waited until dawn if seeing you like this is my reward.* "Raven," he whispered. "You look..."

"Like a grape?" she teased.

He smiled. "Yes. You are the most beautiful and alluring grape I have ever seen."

She laughed. "Such a compliment! However will I resist you, sir?"

He leaned in, levity giving way to desire. "You won't," he said softly. Phillip stepped back, retaining his hold of her hand. "May I have this dance?"

Raven's cheeks blushed as she silently nodded her assent.

He escorted her to the ballroom and marveled at how different the sensation was to enter with Raven on his arm. A hushed ripple of admiration and speculation pooled out around them and every eye turned to see the black haired beauty at his side. Her fingers tightened their grip on his arm and Phillip tried to ease her anxiety. "They are in awe of you, Miss Wells."

She smiled. "They are studying me closely to see if I have some glorious flaw."

"Like a humped back?" he played along.

"It would make for a better gothic tale," she agreed. "If the earl took in some poor scarred and misshapen creature..."

"I'm sure they are just as happy to see a fairy tale princess in their midst."

Raven looked at him askance. "Now who is the optimist?"

He pulled her out onto the marble floor as the musicians began a waltz, and then into his arms. "Dance with me, Raven Wells."

She instinctively relaxed in the circle of his hold, tipping her head back as the world fell away. His eyes were on her and she was transformed into a creature of air and light, the heat from his body surrounding her and shielding her from all care. It was a waltz but she could not hear the music over the beating of her own heart.

Nothing tied her to fear, anxiety over the gossip of her peers as inconsequential as dust. Phillip masterfully guided them through the kaleidoscope of dancers and she forgot to hide her pleasure.

"What are you smiling about, Miss Wells?"

"I am grinning like a fool because all my feminine schemes to impress you with how cool and unaffected I am and how mature I can be; are all for naught! I am giddy, sir, and even knowing how unbecoming it is, I don't care!"

"I like you when you are giddy and it is far more appealing than you suspect." They skirted the far side of the room closest to the open windows and then moved back into the heart of the floor. The music carried them both and he leaned forward slightly to whisper in the sensitive shell of her ear, "Will you come to me again tonight, Raven?"

"Yes!" Raven answered. "I must reward you for the patience you will be forced to show tonight, sir."

"My patience?"

"For I will have to dance with as many men as it takes to repair my reputation after making such a spectacle of myself in your arms," she sighed sweetly. "No one looking at us will fail to notice how I feel about you, Mr. Warrick."

"Good!" It was his turn to laugh. "Let them envy me and by all means, dance with every ugly man in the room if you must. I shall be as patient as a saint."

"Only the ugly ones?" she teased with a pout.

"Very well. Not just the ugly ones. You may also dance with any man over the age of seventy, no matter how handsome he is."

"Phillip!" she protested gently. "Let us say fifty."

"A compromise. Sixty?"

"Sixty it is," she conceded then dared a glance over his shoulder to assess the company. "Oh, dear. There are quite a few men who fall into those categories. I may have overstepped the mark."

"Too late now," he declared. "You will have to make the best of it and I will simply have to do my best to console you later. I will not stay to watch, Miss Wells. I have a good understanding of my limits."

The music ended before she could serve him a saucy reply. Raven curtsied deeply. "Thank you, Mr. Warrick. That was a waltz I shall never forget."

He bowed and then formally escorted her from the floor. Raven was sure that her slippers were not touching the ground. She'd jested about dancing with other men but Raven wasn't completely confident that—

"May I have this dance, Miss Wells?"

She turned to be faced with a man who was neither unattractive nor elderly, but no matter how much she adored her Mr. Warrick; Raven was a young woman at her first dance and she was *not* going to forego her merriment.

"Why, yes! How kind of you!" She took his proffered hand and stole one quick glance at the grim jealous gleam in Phillip's eyes before he retreated from the ballroom. *Good, then. He has my heart and my body, so perhaps it is good for him to simmer a bit.*

The power of her feminine wiles was a heady thing and Raven innocently explored the polite edges of the game as one dance request, became another, and another. Between partners, there was no time to leave the floor until the orchestra finally took a brief pause. Then the competition for glasses of punch and refreshments created a comical rush of men seeking to vie for the honor of bringing her a piece of cake or arguing that a rival had failed to relinquish her quickly enough to allow them to bring her a small iced dessert.

She felt like a lily floating in a pond with dozens of fish nipping at her ankles for attention. By the time Lord Trent appeared, she was grateful for the reprieve. "Come, Raven! Dance with your crusty old guardian and let these men shamelessly fight over your card while we take a turn."

"Gentlemen," she smiled at them apologetically as she took Geoffrey's hand, "if you'll excuse me."

They dramatically lamented her loss and Geoffrey ignored every single one of them to pull her out onto the floor. "God, what have the young men of this country come to? Did that one boy mumble something about surviving on the dew of moonbeams until you returned to his side? Dear Lord! Worst prose in the history of history!"

"Not everyone has your natural gifts, Lord Trent," she demurred. "I heard Lady Baybrook say that you could charm a blackberry bramble into giving you roses if you set your mind to it."

"Ah! I knew I invited that old sow to visit for good reason!" Trent smiled as they turned. "Took her long enough to earn her oats, wouldn't you say?"

She gasped at his humor but took it in stride. "All right then. But let me take this fleeting chance to thank you, your lordship."

"For what?"

"For everything. For tonight, and the silks, and the jewels and… you are generous to me in too many ways to name but I did not want you to think it had gone unnoticed."

His brow furrowed. "Don't turn maudlin. I like it better when you pout about not having enough bonnets, girl."

"Very well. I am happier for having said it."

"And?" he pushed gently.

"And," she gifted him with a wicked smile. "I will make a note to pout and ask you for more things if that is the only thing that pleases you."

"Good girl," Lord Trent nodded. "By the way, I love the way you sent Warrick packing, Raven. He looked as crestfallen as a pup when he left just then."

"Did he?" She swallowed hard, unease creeping across her skin. "I didn't mean to bruise his feelings."

"Are you doing as I've asked, Raven? Are you leading him a merry chase?" he asked.

When did you ask me to lead him on a merry chase?

"I must confess that I—"

"Shhh! Do I look like a priest to you? It's a ball, Raven, and no place for confessions. Besides, I have not forbidden your attachment, have I?"

"No. You didn't." She tried to ignore the sensation that something was wrong. "You thought he would avoid me if he thought I had no dowry but—"

"I don't want to talk about this now, Raven. Besides, I've made such broad hints of your fortunes, perhaps that strategy was useless." He smiled as if they were discussing his favorite dogs. "Do whatever you wish but do not ask me about Warrick again."

"Your lordship?"

The dance ended and he stepped back curtly. "No more talk of Warrick. Don't ruin my evening."

He turned and left her on the floor, a scandalous move since manners dictated that no unmarried woman cross the dance floor alone. Thankfully, one of her admirers swept in to save her and her humiliation was averted. Within minutes, she'd put the incident from her mind for a time. When her new partner stomped on her toes, she laughed and used it as an excuse to pardon herself from the throng.

Raven slipped away to steal a few private moments. She took advantage of one of the servants' doors and walked outside to absorb the cold night's air and admire the view of the glittering party through the windows. By deliberately keeping out of the light's touch on the grass, she knew she was completely invisible to the guests inside.

Can you die from the thrill of giddy social triumph?

Raven hugged her elbows at the notion, wishing that she could clasp this sensation of strange joy tightly enough to keep it forever, to soak it into her bones.

"Are you catching your breath?"

She turned with a gasp at the unfamiliar gravel in the man's voice. "Sir?"

"I am the Duke of Northland." He inclined his snow white covered head a single inch. "At your service."

She curtsied in one graceful motion, trembling at the prospect of meeting such a man out of her element. "Your Grace. I am Raven Wells, ward to the Earl of Trent."

"Charmed. If you are not catching your breath, then are you hiding from some anticipated horror, Miss Wells?"

"What horrors could possibly touch me on a night like this?" she said with a smile. "You are too melancholy, Your Grace."

He smiled, stepping out from the shadows but not entirely embracing the light from the room. "Am I?"

She nodded, the euphoria dancing still clouding her senses. "As your reputation demands, I expect."

"How did he manage it? In one gentle frame to have raised a creature so wild and so adept at the trappings of civilization?"

She pressed her fingertips to her cheeks. "I spoke without censure!"

"It is your youth that speaks so and it is your greatest asset. But then youth would also be your greatest weakness. I allude to horror and you deny its existence. God," he let out a soft sigh, "may life never teach you the error in that."

"I—I did not hear you announced and my guardian and your host, Lord Trent would be mortified to think I'd met such a peer while I was hiding out on the lawn."

The duke shook his head. "I am not expected. He invites me to everything but I, I never attend. Anything. As my reputation demands."

Raven tipped her head to one side to take a different measure of the man. The mysterious Duke of Northland had been more of a ghostly figure than anything else for as long as she could remember.

She'd seen his name on a card on her guardian's desk years ago and Geoffrey had forbidden her to speak his name aloud. But the duke was on every guest list that Lord Trent kept. Their correspondence was always under lock and key and provided more security than any treasure or trinket in the house.

But here he was. A man, after all, and not a ghost.

"I should have recognized you, Your Grace."

"How is that, Miss Wells?" he asked.

"Two years ago, I was in Strathmore to visit a friend of Trent's and to shop when your carriage stopped on a journey to London I imagine. It caused quite a stir. Just your coat of arms on the carriage door was enough to send every woman who possessed a decent gown scurrying for her powders."

"Did they indeed?"

"I'll admit I was as eager as any to see what a duke looks like."

"Did I disappoint?"

It was an open invitation for flattery that she ignored, not out of malice but simply because she didn't think someone as elevated as a duke had much need for the convention. "You weren't what I expected but I don't think it's possible to disappoint when even your footmen have gilt on their sleeves."

"What did you expect to see in a duke?"

"I don't wish to say."

Silence was his reproach and she relented with a small twinge of misery. "Very well but before I answer I wish to say that of all the meetings with a duke I had envisioned, none of my fantasies included me making such a muck and mess of it!"

"Understood."

"I thought you would be much taller and not quite as chubby," she confessed miserably. "And while the livery was very shiny, you were wearing the dullest waistcoat I've ever seen. There. I'm made despicable."

"I love your honesty."

His voice caught and Raven was stilled by a strange flash of emotion in his eyes. "Your Grace?"

"Tell me what my reputation demands, Miss Wells. What kind of man am I?"

"You are…as unknown to me as a star in the heavens, Your Grace. As far above me and as distant, I'm afraid to say. But imagination and rumor takes hold and I have only heard whispers of a lonely man who rarely ventures out into the world that he is the master of."

"Am I a cruel man?" he asked.

She stared at him in shock at the question. Eyes the color of gray smoke like her own reflected only pain and without thinking she reached out a gloved hand to touch his arm. "Never! No one could think it! And if they claimed such a thing, I would amend their opinion with my own!"

"And what is your opinion to counter theirs?"

"That whatever has driven you from the world, must have been terrible, indeed and…that it is not our place to judge such a great man. I am no one, Your Grace. Truly. But if a girl who is nothing can befriend an element in the heavens, I hope you will accept my care."

"How did he manage it?" His smile lacked warmth and never touched the agony in his eyes as he retreated from her touch. "I never thought to meet you, my dear but I am glad that my reason was overruled by my curiosity. I wanted to see Trent's ward for myself."

"Your Grace?"

"Good evening, Miss Wells."

"Good evening, Your Grace," she said, and curtseyed again, well aware that her audience with him had come to an end and that there was no argument or amendments she could make before he turned on his heels and left without another word.

I cannot believe I spoke so boldly to a duke!

And that he still manages to wear the most dreadful waistcoats I have ever seen…

CHAPTER 15

She'd left Phillip's bed just before dawn and he awoke more determined than ever to end the secrecy that enveloped them both. Clandestine romances were all well and good, but he was convinced that Trent would not appreciate their deception.

Well, that and the sight of her like a glorious flower with all those pesky male bees around her...

He waited in the dining room for his host to emerge and was finally rewarded closer to the lunch hour than breakfast. "Good morning, your lordship."

The earl held up his hand as if to ward off cheer. "Not so loud, dear boy. God, what was I thinking? After wounding myself on our little hunt with all that whiskey, why in the world would I think to stupidly sample all that punch?"

So much for catching him in a good mood to talk.

"The evening was a triumph," Phillip said levelly, lowering his voice slightly to earn a smile from his host.

"Yours certainly was!" Trent tapped his cup and was instantly provided with a steaming cup of black coffee by one of the footmen. "Mrs. Pratt confided that her daughter is completely in love after you honored her with a quadrille."

"Gracious! As quick as that!" Phillip took a bite of eggs. "A shame I don't even remember the girl and I sure as hell didn't dance a quadrille. Perhaps she has lost her heart to Mr. Sheffield?"

"Are you not going to even ask what her dowry entails before you throw her over?"

Phillip shook his head. "No."

Trent shook his head. "A sad state of affairs! Clementine Pratt has tits the size of watermelons and a dowry to match! Where is your enthusiasm for the hunt?"

"I am not hunting." Phillip put his fork down. "When a man finds what he wants, he doesn't keep searching."

"A common mistake." Trent attacked his toast with vigor. "Who knows what diamonds of the first water are missed once a man blinds himself to his choices?

"Your lordship," Phillip started again. "My devotion to—"

"Warrick. My head hurts. Slow and steady." Geoffrey held up a toast point to accent his words. "Rome was not built in a day."

"Of course. And if I were building Rome..." Phillip sighed. "As you wish. But I want to talk to you about Raven before the holiday is over and I will not be dissuaded."

"Plenty of time," Trent said with a sigh. "Raven is special and I'm sure you're already aware that I have placed a great deal of store by her happiness."

"Of course. But Raven's happiness is something that I crave as well and would do anything to achieve."

Trent grimaced. "Easy to make a woman happy. It is keeping them happy that has perplexed many a man! But let's leave the subject. Raven will ultimately decide for herself. She is young and there is time enough to debate what merits will win both her and her dowry."

Phillip sighed with relief. Even if he hadn't secured the man's blessings, he'd finally moved the topic further down the field and gotten Trent to agree to talk later.

Or at least, let's hope that's what he meant...

"Ah, Mr. Sheffield! Worst dancing I have ever witnessed!" Trent proclaimed. "What cheers you this morning?"

Mr. Sheffield wisely ignored his host's jest. "Lord Morley and I challenged several men to a friendly game of cards and it was extremely rewarding! I'm sorry you missed the chance, Warrick."

"I didn't miss the chance. I don't gamble, Mr. Sheffield."

The earl rolled his eyes. "He doesn't gamble, Mr. Sheffield. He doesn't cavort. And he certainly doesn't notice the finest set of breasts to ever grace the British Isles. Mr. Warrick is a fortress of morality."

Mr. Sheffield grinned like an ape at him over his plate of sausages. "Is that so?"

Lord Morley strolled in before Phillip could fire back. "God, what a night! The quiet of the country is an elusive prize and I am beginning to think our host has deliberately kept it from our reach this entire time!"

"I thought you had a rousing card game last night," Trent countered. "Or is it only Mr. Sheffield's purse that gained in weight?"

"I did well enough," Lord Morley conceded. "Here! Coffee, here!" he tapped on his cup soundly nearly tipping it over.

"God, Morley! Did you injure your hand?" Trent asked. "Your knuckles are scraped to hell."

"Merely a rash," Morley replied. "Nothing as contagious as leprosy so not a concern, gentlemen."

"Poor man!" Sheffield said. "A hot bath in salts may see you through it."

Morley's brow furrowed, his lip curling. "Salts? In open wounds? Thank goodness you have not applied yourself to the profession of a physician! Your patients would run mad with your 'tender ministrations.'"

Phillip joined in the general laughter and then excused himself as the conversation turned back toward the men's winnings at cards.

He headed back out toward the main hall only to spot Raven heading toward a hidden door set beneath the stairs. Something in the furtive way she lifted the latch to the door caught his attention.

"Raven."

"Oh!" She straightened guiltily but then smiled as she approached him. "What a...pleasant surprise to find you up and about!" She lowered her voice and leaned forward, "And looking so refreshed after getting so little sleep."

"I could say the same for you, Miss Wells." It was not empty praise. Raven Wells' eyes were bright and her countenance as clear as the day he'd arrived. Hours of passion had energized her where another woman would have been drained. He shook his head in astonished admiration. "I didn't think to see you before dinner."

She blushed. "I didn't think to open my eyes before sunset but... perhaps it is the excitement of the dance? The lingering after-effects of a glorious night?"

Frustration edged his awakening senses. In another time and place, he would have happily put her over his shoulder and carried her back upstairs for another round of sensual pursuits. But the 'fortress of morality' was all too aware of the constraints of the day. "What door is this?"

She answered him as she deliberately moved away from the portal. "One of the servant's passages."

"What were you doing there?" he asked.

She crossed her arms. "Nothing that requires questioning, Mr. Warrick. I wished a word with Mr. Walters and the housekeeper to convey my compliments on the staff's hard work. I didn't want my guardian to catch me as he rarely bothers to praise anyone in his employ. But I think it is important to—"

"Whoa!" He reached out to gently touch her arm. "I overstepped. It is not my place to question you, Raven."

"No. It is not," she agreed with a shy smile.

"And I should have guessed your mission would have some philanthropic theme."

"Yes. I am practically a saint." The smile gave way to laughter and he risked a quick kiss on the tip of her nose before stepping back firmly.

"I did not mean to interfere."

"Thank you, Phillip." She walked back to the portal and then hesitated. "Please say nothing to the earl."

He nodded. "Your secret is safe with me."

"Thank you," she said softly, smiling at him before Raven quickly disappeared through the doorway.

The lady vanishes and I think I will crawl upstairs and sleep while I can.

Rome wasn't built in a day but I have the growing feeling I'm going to need all the strength I can muster before the earl threatens to toss me to the lions.

* * *

SHE HATED KEEPING secrets from Phillip, but her vow to Lady Morley was paramount. Mrs. Lindstrom had sent word that Millicent had suffered another bout with her "cold". Raven hadn't wished to risk being caught in her friend's bedroom and had gone below stairs to talk to Kitty and learn more about how the lady fared.

She pulled a handful of buttons from her skirt pocket as she made her way down the narrow stairs.

"Oh, Miss Wells!" One of the footmen stepped aside, astonished to see her in the passage.

"I was looking for Miss Polk. I found the buttons I want for my new daydress."

His confusion was obvious. "I can see them to her if you'd prefer, Miss Wells."

"I would rather do it myself. Besides, after last night, it is the least I can do to save someone the effort of climbing the stairs over a trifle."

"You are very kind to think of it, miss."

She nodded and moved past him, praying that if anyone else questioned her presence, she would have an ally.

Within minutes, she found Kitty in the servant's common room. "Miss Polk, do you have a moment to spare?"

"Of course," Kitty stood from the table and set her sewing aside to follow Raven into the quiet hallway.

"Is there somewhere we can talk privately?"

"This way." Kitty lead her through the labyrinth of the manor's service areas of the house, past the kitchens and then up yet another narrow set of stairs to the maidservants' rooms. "Here. Come in here."

Raven took in the meager accommodations, struck by the bleak lack of color and decorations. "Are you comfortable here, Kitty?"

Kitty tapped her foot, her hands fisted at her hips. "Did you come all the way down here to inspect my room, Raven Wells?"

"No," Raven said and forced herself to focus on the matter at hand. "Lady Morley is...unwell again."

"Mrs. Lindstrom was as pale as a sheet this morning, so I knew as much even before she told me."

"How bad is it?"

"Bad enough but Mrs. Lindstrom said she's seen worse."

Raven smoothed her curls from her forehead. "It's a nightmare. Did you make more salve?"

"I did, though this time he was too cunning to mar her face. He's hiding his handiwork to try to keep you well out of it, miss."

"I hate that man, Kitty."

"Course you do. My ma always says just make sure that if you hate someone you aren't surprised when they hate you back."

"Oh, there is no doubt he returns the sentiments!" Raven waved it off. "I'm not afraid of him."

Kitty refolded the quilt on her bed. "That man is a piece of work the devil is probably sorry to claim!"

"Will she be down for dinner tonight?"

"I'll find out."

"Thank you, Kitty. I don't know what I would do without you!"

"Miss Wells? Mind me asking where you got to last night?"

"What?"

"Well, I doubled back after I helped you unlace because I recalled I'd forgotten to pull the drapes and...you were nowhere to be found."

"I...can't tell you." Raven held out the buttons. "Here. Take these. An excuse for our meeting."

Kitty took them from her, her gaze never dropping. "I like Mr. Warrick. Just mind yourself. The earl...he has no fondness for that man."

"I know, Kitty. I know!" She smiled and kissed her maid's cheek before fleeing Kitty's well-meant words. "I have it all in hand, Miss Polk!"

Kitty sat down slowly on her bed, clutching the jet buttons and prayed that her Raven was right.

CHAPTER 16

*D*inner that night was a subdued affair as most of the conversation reviewed the successes of the ball or lamented the lack of sleep. Lady Morley showed no sign of injury but Raven was grateful for her presence. Millicent avoided looking at her friend. Raven deliberately waited until the dessert was served before she brought up her last proposal for the holiday.

"There are only a few days left before everyone leaves," Raven said clearly enough for her voice to carry to the entire table. "But perhaps there is time for one more planned diversion?"

"I would say not," Lord Morley said firmly. "Or I will forfeit my next country holiday for the dull pace of the city!"

The earl laughed. "Damn it, Morley! You are consistent! I'll give you that much!" He waved his spoon like a scepter toward Raven. "Pray, continue!"

"I was thinking that it would be lovely to provide a memorable finish to the holiday."

"Oh, I hope so!" Mrs. Carlton said quickly. "Though it has already been one of the most memorable country parties of my life."

Raven looked at Mr. Warrick and their gazes locked. "Days and nights I will treasure for as long as I live," Phillip said softly.

Mr. Carlton took his wife's hand with a tender smile. "I agree." He glanced at his host and his ward. "Your hospitality has no equal."

"There you have it," the earl sighed and leaned back against his chair. "Raven, you will have to rise to the challenge and come up with something unique and unforgettable if you are to deliver a fitting grand finale to this holiday!"

"I propose a theatrical evening!" Raven said forcing herself to look away from Phillip's heated gaze. "Nothing too polished, but what fun if the ladies put on a small performance of scenes for the gentlemen's amusement." As Lord Morley began to clear his throat to protest, she quickly added, "Nothing scandalous or unseemly! I was thinking a few short snippets from Shakespeare to edify our souls and only scenes that my guardian approves!"

"I love Shakespeare!" the earl said enthusiastically. "And what fun to watch the women muddle through the classics! Though I shall insist that all of you make a complete effort. No half-hearted squeaks if you are performing 'King Lear'!"

Mrs. Carlton grew pale. "Oh, my! I am hardly one for public speaking."

Lady Baybrook rolled her eyes. "As if anyone would give you a role requiring a thunderous presence."

"Then it is clear that Lady Baybrook shall be sure to recite the meatier and more royal parts," Trent noted. "I am already anticipating your glorious performance, your ladyship."

Raven added, "That is…if you will agree to participate in our humble offerings."

"I suppose I could—if there is no nonsense in the scene I am assigned! I shall approach it as a dignified reading and not make a scandalous theatrical display of myself." Lady Baybrook took a small sip of her wine to hide a smile. "In my youth, I was often asked to read aloud for my beautiful voice."

"And Lady Morley?" Mrs. Carlton asked. "Are you disposed to play?"

Millicent looked at her husband, waiting to see his reaction before answering, but Lord Trent pounded his hand on the table.

"Of course, she is up for it!" the earl pronounced. "Come, Morley, bid your wife to perform for I tell you, it'll be a poor showing without her don't you think?"

"I'm not sure it is proper..." Lord Morley began but his words faded as the dowager Lady Baybrook's eyebrows lifted in disapproval at the objection since she had already agreed to it. "Millicent is unskilled."

"It's an amateur theatrical," Lord Trent said firmly. "And no one assumed she is a grand actress, old boy. Don't be ridiculous! That's what makes it amusing! No offense ladies, but the satire of watching you butcher the ethereal language of the Bard will likely warm my toes for many months and years to come."

Raven blushed but bravely continued. "We may surprise you, Lord Trent."

"If Millicent wishes to risk humiliation, then I won't forbid it," Lord Morley said grudgingly.

"Lady Morley?" Trent looked at her.

She nodded happily. "I would love to try."

"Then it's settled!" The earl struck the table again and the crystal rang obediently. "Let's have it ready for Thursday night since everyone is slated to leave within a day or two afterward."

"Yes, that sounds perfect." Raven agreed. "We'll begin our rehearsals tomorrow."

"Three days." Mrs. Carlton fanned herself with her hand. "Please tell me we are not memorizing our lines!"

"If you apply yourself, Mrs. Carlton," Lady Baybrook said archly, "I'm sure you can accomplish it. My concerns lie with the far weightier challenges of my costume. I expect we will not be wearing shapeless sack cloths, Miss Wells."

"No, Lady Baybrook. With Lord Trent's permission, I will enlist the help of the house staff to accomplish all. Masks, costumes and sets, will all be provided and sure to exceed your expectations, your ladyship." Raven smiled.

"Good!" the earl signaled an end to the meal. "Let's allow the ladies to retreat to begin their scheming as I for one, am ready for a splash of brandy!"

Lady Baybrook rose first and all the women followed her lead to yield the dining room to the men.

CHAPTER 17

*L*ater that night in the sanctuary of his room, Phillip enticed her to join him for a small taste of sherry before they retired. "A theatrical evening?" he asked as he held out her glass.

"You do not approve, Mr. Warrick?" Raven took it, sniffed the sweet and potent spirit only to wrinkle her nose at the assault on her delicate sensibilities. She set the crystal on the table without tasting it.

He smiled at her refusal and focused instead on the topic at hand. "I approve. Honestly, I approve a bit too much for when you said it all I could envision was you wearing some diaphanous thing as Juliet to my Romeo, bidding me to kiss you."

"Did you?" Raven held up her hand to his, her smaller fingers warming the sensitive pads of his. "And?"

"If I profane with my unworthiest hand this holy shrine, the gentle fine is this—my lips, two blushing pilgrims, ready stand to smooth that rough touch with a tender kiss." Phillip struggled to keep from grinning as he wrestled up the lines from some dusty vault inside of his head, thanking a long forgotten tutor for the lesson.

"Good pilgrim, you do wrong your hand too much," Raven said and planted a wicked kiss on the palm of his hand, her tongue darting out to touch the sensitive well tracing the subtle lines there.

"Oh, hell!" Phillip sighed. "Now I can't remember any of it."

"No? Not even...Thus from my lips, by yours, my sin is purged?" She kissed the outer slope of his neck, trailing hot sweet paths up to finally nip at his earlobe. "Not event that part?"

He tried again. "Sin from my lips? O trespass sweetly urged! Give me my sin again!"

He bent over to kiss her, the warm velvet of her mouth making him feel drunk. She clung to his shoulders and Phillip reveled in her touch because he was a giant holding wildfire in his arms. It was magic. He lifted his head to look down into her eyes, confident of his prowess.

"You kiss by the book." It was the next line but the tease was so perfect, Raven hoped Shakespeare didn't mind their wicked play.

"By the book?" His eyebrows knit together in dismay. "And how would you rather kiss me, Raven Wells?"

Ever since Phillip had undone her so thoroughly the other night, Raven had been gathering her courage. For if he was her masculine mirror, then she longed to gift him with the pleasure of her mouth. He had already taught her how he liked to be touched, so the leap was not too far for her desire to make.

She trailed her fingertips down his shirt front slowly dropping downward until her touch skirted the buttons of his breeches. His flesh was already thickening and the weight of it aided her as the buttons gave away easily. She freed him to take in the raw beauty of his arousal. She loved this part of his anatomy, not only for its delicious power and ability to please, but for the way it responded to her lightest touch. It was as if it had a mind and heart of its own, and as if Raven had them both to master.

"Raven," he said softly, his jaw clenched to make it a growl betraying his needs.

She ran her fingers along the silken length, gripping and measuring him, firmly enough to make speech useless as he reached a hand out to steady himself against the table.

She knelt before him, her skirts spreading out around her and knew that she had stumbled onto something magical. She leaned forward, still working his flesh, drawing him out and dragging her fingernails lightly underneath his shaft until he moaned. She kissed him, tasting his ripe head against her tongue and savoring the sweet musk and salt of the pearl of moisture she evoked from his body. Her mouth enclosed him and pulled him slowly into the pocket there, her tongue lathing the sensitive juncture under the swollen tip, flicking and pressing into his flesh the way he had teased and worked the flesh between her thighs.

If kissing him was a sin, she was happy to drown in the glorious feelings that coursed through her. Phillip's hips moved of their own accord, pressing forward to give her more of him before he retreated and robbed her of her feast. He lifted her to her feet and carried her without another word to the bed. Clothing flew fast and Raven found herself on her hands and knees on the bed, his thighs against hers, and the cock she had worshipped was poised to fill her completely.

"Yes!" she sighed. "Please, darling, hurry!"

He obeyed but rebelliously as slow as he could manage. Inch by inch, he generously gave her what she demanded but at a pace that he controlled.

"Phillip!" she protested.

"Shh! I want to prove that not everything has to come at a gallop."

She threw her head back, and was finally rewarded as her body stretched to accommodate him, their limits edging them both toward the finish. Raven cried out as she began to shatter, the quick tangle of her pending release catching her off guard.

But Phillip mercifully shifted them both to land squarely in the bed, moving with her so that she was beneath him again, her legs wrapped around his waist with her ankles pressing into his lower back, driving him on. He rode her, each stroke a lazy study in memorizing their desires and Raven sighed at the dream of it.

"Oh, Phillip! I am glad that we are not Romeo and Juliet! But can we be this happy and not fear?"

"Our houses are hardly divided. Let us hope to end better, my beauty."

"Lord Trent is sure to give you his consent."

"I have to ask him tomorrow."

"Please. Please wait until after the theatrical performances on Thursday night. There is a…matter I must see to. Then I will feel free to pursue my own permanent happiness and my instincts tell me that after our play, my dear guardian will be grateful and relieved to know that I have met my match."

"Grateful and relieved? Raven, what are you up to?"

"I am asking you to trust me. Do you trust me, Phillip?"

He nodded slowly. "Trust you? You have me, lady. Everything I am and all I hold dear appears to be in these beautiful little hands." He kissed her fingertips, his tender gesture transforming into a sensual assault that unfurled raw longing inside of her.

Those beautiful little hands began to itch to touch him. "Phillip," she whispered. "I am too restless for a tender game. Please. I wish to be ruined."

Ruin came in a passionate blaze and leisure was left behind. Raven matched him, his every move, his every thrust was met with her eager hips, her sensual hands and the magic of her mouth against any part of him she could reach. The frenzy of their coupling overtook them both at the same time and when Raven cried out her release, he covered her mouth with his own and exhaled a groan as his climax matched hers.

She was sustenance and light, and Phillip was humbled at the force of his climax. Orgasm knifed from his body and he clung to her until the waves of ecstasy passed and allowed him to breath again.

They stayed in the tangle of his bed to smooth each other's skin and playfully extend the contact.

"Am I too forward, Phillip?"

He shook his head. "So long as your boldness is reserved only for me, I cannot find fault."

"You alone—inspire such a fire in me that I am terrified sometimes. I am a glutton when it comes to you, and surely that is not an attractive thing, Phillip. Perhaps that is why there is so much said of refraining from indulgence in carnal desires. For I swear, from that first kiss in the gazebo until, yes, even until this moment, I am in an eternal fever for you, sir. It is ridiculous! Is this what you meant to warn me about? Have you experience with this malady?"

He shook his head, biting the inside of his cheek to keep from smiling. "I thought I had but I was wrong. I have fallen victim to the same state of addiction, Miss Wells. Whatever I knew of the connection between a man and a woman has faded into useless and forgotten noise." He lowered his lips to glide down the firm outer lines of her neck, teasing the sensitive juncture at her shoulder. "This is a love I have never known."

Raven sighed in contentment, yielding yet again to his touch. "Then let us never recover from it, my love."

"Never, my heart."

CHAPTER 18

*T*hey took advantage of the fine weather the following morning and Raven brought along her speech written out for the theatrical, to study her lines. On the long cushioned seat, he lay with his head in her lap while she read her piece over and over.

"I hate the growing feeling that I'm in a play, Raven, but that I don't know my lines."

"Truly?" she asked.

"Time is running out. Your guardian's mood is too erratic to chart and I'm worried that even your glittering night of readings is not going to make a dent." Phillip closed his eyes. "I should speak to him this afternoon."

Raven hit him lightly with her paper, enjoying the playful swish and pop of it against his nose. "Do you doubt my talents on the stage, sir? We will charm all of you into happy beasts and the plan will work. You'll see. Have a little faith, my love."

"This has nothing to do with faith. If his mood is level enough today or at any time before Friday arrives, why not make the most of it?" Phillip asked and then captured her wrist. "And no more swatting. I am abused enough as it stands."

"You are hardly a bruised and cowering soul!" she laughed. "But I will be more gentle with you, sir. I am no bully."

Phillip sat up slowly. "You are not a bully but I have to admire the way you get what you want. How is it that I lose every debate?"

"What debate?" she asked.

"Trent is difficult to persuade on his best days. Tell me again why I am waiting to approach him? Does this not make us look less and less well-intentioned? It will be harder to argue my honorable nature and good character when I am clearly the villain in this."

"You are no villain, Phillip. You could never be a villain."

"Raven. I have to take ownership of what I've done or that is precisely what I will be. If I am not an honest man who can admit to his mistakes, then I am a villain who hides the truth."

It was a poor choice of words and he regretted it instantly.

"His mistakes?" Her grey eyes darkened with the insult. "Have you made an error in bedding me?"

"Not a mistake! But a—damn it, Raven. The order is not what the rules of society dictate, and even you who enjoy playing the wild and carefree girl when it suits you; even you have to admit that it is a fault in both our characters to give in to the passion between us before marriage!"

"Oh!" She stood to stamp one small foot in her fury. "I hate the rules of society! And I especially hate the rules of society when they demean my feelings for the man I love and make him use words like 'mistake' and 'fault' to relate what I shall defend to my grave as raw perfection!"

Phillip was stunned at her anger but also at how beautiful she was when riled. It was all he could do to nod. "I apologize. I am very grateful for my slice of raw perfection, Miss Wells."

She forgot her recent pledge not to bruise him and punched his shoulder with a touch more vigor. "You should be! You bleak lump of a man!" Her fingers flew to her lips and her eyes widened in horror. "Oh! I'm—sorry. But if you only knew the terror you invoke when you..."

"Raven," he stood to pull her into his arms, her ear nesting against his heartbeat. "I am a very, very lucky bleak lump of a man. I only want to make things right with Trent and secure this raw perfection between us. Doesn't that make sense?"

She nodded and leaned back to look up at him. "Of course it does. But I—I cannot take the chance until after the performance. If he tosses us out..." she shuddered at the thought.

If he throws me out then I will have abandoned Lady Morley and my promise to her. I wouldn't be able to live with myself if my happiness came at the cost of hers. But I can't explain any of it to you, my love. Not without destroying her faith in me.

Oh, god—what a mess!

"Are you afraid of him, Raven?"

She shook her head. "No! It isn't that. Do not misunderstand. He may roar when the time comes...or be as mild as a lamb at the news, but neither reaction changes my feelings for you, Phillip."

"Then why wait for—"

"No! No! No!" Raven pulled away from him, distress making her voice rough and uneven. "I will not be drawn into this again. It is Wednesday, Phillip Warrick. I ask you to wait until after tomorrow night's performance. Is that such a weighty request? Must I give you a dozen sound reasons and defend my position repeatedly?"

"Perhaps not," he conceded.

"It is a matter of faith. Either you believe in me, Phillip, or you do not. Which is it?" Raven asked and then held her breath.

"I believe in you, Raven Wells."

Relief brought tears to her eyes. "And I believe in you."

He took her hands into his and kissed her fingertips, a penitent soul. "After the performance. You have my word."

"Thank you, Phillip!" She pulled herself up by his lapels to balance on her tip toes to kiss him. "Thank you."

He lifted her into his arms, deepening the kiss and abandoning all arguments.

Raven rewarded him with all the enthusiasm her spirit possessed and silently vowed that after Friday, she would let him win every debate that married life might provide to make it up to him for her deception.

* * *

THAT AFTERNOON, a game of croquet on the south lawn sprang up and the entire party ended up embroiled in the tournament, although some as spectators and not directly as players. Phillip had triumphed in the first round and would have volunteered to partner with Raven, but Lord Trent hailed him to come over to his table.

"Your Lordship? Did you wish to jump in?" Phillip asked.

"No. But come, I wish to take a walk and there is nothing worse than rattling away to oneself so I am asking you to come with me."

"For conversation then?"

The earl laughed. "No! So that you can make it look like a conversation when I rattle on to myself, dear boy!"

"Of course," he said, sending a quick look of apology to Raven as he set his mallet aside. "How can I refuse such a unique invitation?"

The others waved them merrily away while Raven watched them go with an anxious look. Phillip knew she feared that he would break his promise but he was resolute to prove that he could stay the course.

"Did you enjoy your time at Oakwell Manor, Warrick?"

"Very much," Phillip answered, aware that the earl was setting out on the lake path. It was an irony that would test him but Phillip kept his hands tightly clasped behind his back. "You are very blessed with the beauty of your estates."

"I am," Trent agreed.

They walked in silence for a few minutes before the earl spoke again. "Oakwell Manor is as timeless as the land itself. But then, I get a little melancholy to think that life is such a fleeting thing and that the house looks on as I barely pass through—without much impact."

"You've preserved it and kept it whole. I'd say that's impact enough in these troubled times." Phillip spoke from sincere admiration. "So many have lost their fortunes in the uproar of railroad schemes and foreign treasure hunts, but you've stayed above the fray and done well for yourself—and your descendants. I'm sure your efforts won't be forgotten."

"Oh, well, there is that, isn't there?" the earl picked up a long stick to prod the ground and part the grasses as they strolled along. "Never mind. Talking about legacies is like rambling about the stars. They are all well and good but they never really touch us."

Phillip smiled at the practicality of the man but Trent's steps immediately stopped.

"Are you laughing at me, Warrick? You think I'm some maudlin and weak old man?" he demanded.

"No. Not at all. I was only marveling that such a grounded and no-nonsense man could raise a woman who seems barely tethered to this world." Phillip said, suddenly unsure of where things had gone wrong.

"I am capable of many things you cannot fathom," Trent said calmly and then continued walking as if all was well between them.

Phillip said nothing, falling in step beside his host and friend.

Trent's shoulders relaxed as they approached the water. "I love this view of the house."

Oh, I remember the view...a little too well.

Phillip could see the glade in the corner of his eye and did his best to keep his breathing even. "It's like a painting."

"You are a new man, Sir Warrick. So restrained and disciplined. I admire this version of you." Trent tossed his stick in the water. "I confess I suspected that you had only come here in some greedy clasping scheme to earn my confidence for your financial gain. Can you imagine?"

Damn. Restrained and disciplined would not be the words I expect you to apply come Friday...and that guess of my original motives comes close enough for a shave.

Phillip nodded. "I can."

"But you've not so much as tugged on my coattails for details about my next venture." Trent smiled broadly. "Bravo!"

Phillip held his ground and decided that he could keep his promise to Raven but still salvage what self respect he could. "You're mocking me, aren't you? You know I'd have happily pursued any business you'd invited me to discuss. You were testing me, I think."

"Perhaps. Tests are good for the soul, Warrick."

"Did I pass or fail?"

"We'll see," Trent said enigmatically and then moved to continue walking down the path. "We'll see."

BY THE TIME Trent left him after their hike, Phillip decided to steal a few minutes for himself. The lavender was in full bloom and Phillip traced the long rows, the droning song of the bees underlining his thoughts.

There was no clear answer with Lord Trent and Phillip wrestled with the guilt of inflicting a painful scene on Raven when Friday came. Her optimism was endearing but every fiber of his being blazed a warning that the earl would not relinquish his "treasure" without a squabble.

It would sting, but he did not think the wounds could be fatal to any involved. He would find a way to appease Lord Trent, but he worried that Raven's spirit would bear the brunt of any tension.

He was resigned to spending every waking hour left to him to compose his best case for Trent, lying by omission as much as he could stomach.

He looked up at a few gathering clouds in the sky and smiled.

I am a man transformed. God help me, she has changed me so completely I hardly recognize myself.

He had never been the kind of man to grin at the empty air and daydream of the magical appeal of one woman's laughter, but here he was. A dizzy fool so deeply in love he was humming all the time, putting his coats on inside out and making poor Timms question his sanity. And when he asked Trent for her hand, if the earl started babbling about the advantages of prunes over plums, Phillip was ready to dig in and hold his ground.

Suddenly, his chin dropped as a small detail he'd completely forgotten fell back into his thoughts. "Damn it! I'm almost out of time!"

He raced back into the manor house and rang for Timms, breathless and agitated, only to find the man upstairs in his room already setting out his clothes for the evening.

"Timms?"

"Yes, sir." Mr. Timms held out two sets of cufflinks. "Neither for tonight, then? Shall I get the enamel pair with the silver inlay?"

"No, these are fine." He made his selection without really looking. "Is there a jeweler in the village?"

"A jeweler?" Timms echoed in surprise. "A proper jeweler?"

"Yes. Is there a proper jeweler in the village?"

"Mr. Sinclair is a goldsmith and has a lovely little shop next to the milliner's. But the earl generally sends off to London for his—"

"Thank you, Timms." Phillip straightened his shoulders. "I need my horse brought out and saddled. I think I'll go out for a bit of exercise this morning. Are my riding clothes at hand?"

"They are—let me just pull them quickly and fetch your boots. I'd collected them for a polish and left them downstairs, so I apologize."

"No apologies," Phillip clapped him on the shoulder. "Mr. Timms, I have the grand feeling that I will never again complain in my lifetime."

"My! As grand as that? I'll hurry all the more, sir! Never will I let it be said that I dampened or even foiled such a rare miracle," Mr. Timms said with all seriousness and left Phillip to enjoy the moment.

Mr. Sinclair, let's see if I can rely on your discretion.

And hell, even if I can't, then I've kept my word to Raven and just brought things to a head a day or two earlier than planned. If heaven is secured sooner rather than later, who am I to complain?

Phillip laughed out loud and stretched his arms wide to embrace the dizzying happiness that the future held for him—for there was nothing between him and paradise.

CHAPTER 19

"Why am I so scattered?" Mrs. Carlton asked breathlessly. "My goodness, every line has evaporated from my mind!"

"Why did the earl invite his neighbors to this?" Lady Morley moaned, her nerves betraying her as her voice shook. "I thought to do this before such a small gathering but there must be twenty people out there!"

Raven took Millicent's hand for a quick squeeze. "The earl is proud of our efforts and wishes to make it known. Take heart, Lady Morley."

"I am not exaggerating. I cannot remember my own name!" Mrs. Carlton lamented.

"Dear Mrs. Carlton," Raven said before kissing the woman's cheek. "Mr. Carlton has already proclaimed that he will applaud your Marc Antony if you were to recite the entire monologue in reverse. What is there to fear?"

"Well, when you put it like that…I cannot really disappoint, can I?"

"There! Besides if you forget a line, remember that Mr. Walters is standing by with the pages to gently prompt you." Raven peeked out to where the butler stood at the ready. "I swear, he was so thrilled to be asked, I fear he might jump in to prompt you whether you need it or not."

"I have no need for a prompter," Lady Baybrook said. "Miss Wells, is the gold trim on my cloak showing to its advantage? I asked that maid to make sure that it was a regal amount of cording but now that I see it again, I am unsure."

"It is an intimate setting, your ladyship, and I have to say, the cloak is stunning in the candlelight. You are—breathtaking." Raven turned to make another check of the costumes. "Very well, we are nearly ready to start. Lady Baybrook will do us the honor of leading off, then Lady Morley's Lady Macbeth, Mrs. Carlton's piece from Julius Ceasar, my performance and then we shall all regroup for our piece from "A Midsummer's Night's Dream". Remember to change into your costumes for that final piece as you finish your own. We will all aid each other in that."

"What if they laugh?" Mrs. Carlton asked, her grip on her gold painted staff tightening.

"Then we will be very pleased with ourselves for providing for their merriment," Raven replied. "Ladies, enough. Latch your courage to the sticking place and let's enjoy ourselves."

She signaled the start of their performance and Lady Baybrook strolled out to begin, to the happy applause of the small audience. Raven took the narrow opportunity to turn to Lady Morley and drew her aside while Mrs. Carlton watched Lady Baybrook in rapt attention.

"Are you ready?"

"I am." Millicent tried to smile but failed. "Is everything...set?"

"Everything."

Lady Morley embraced her, a spontaneous hold that steadied them both. "I will never be able to thank you enough for—"

"There is no need. Come, let's give them a show that they will never forget."

The library had been converted into a makeshift theatre, thanks to the carved arches the center columns provided. A curtain of red cloth was strung on a cord across the span dividing the room into two partitions for performers and their audience. Chairs had been added to accommodate an eager if small crowd. Mr. Walters was stationed to the left of the curtains with a small podium, a proud and visible prompter at the ready.

Expectations were truly for nothing more than an amateur pass at so lofty a goal and the earl was quick to tell his neighbors that the ladies had barely had a few days to prepare as if to buffer criticism. Phillip marveled at how anxious the man seemed, as if the opinions of the local gentry was all encompassing when he had only the night before made some comment about not giving a fig for anyone's view but his own.

Male guests of Oakwell Manor enjoyed a place of honor in their front row chairs, with the earl front and center, like a king about to take in a performance at his command. Phillip settled in next to Mr. Carlton and waited patiently for things to begin.

Mr. Carlton leaned over to whisper, "If my wife doesn't faint, I shall dub it a Complete Triumph."

"I say it is a Complete Triumph if she even walks out, sir, considering how shy she is. How proud you must be for her to even make this attempt!" Phillip replied softly. "I see it as a demonstration of her love for you, Mr. Carlton, and nothing less."

"I need no demonstration, Mr. Warrick." Mr. Carlton sighed in contentment. "Love never need prove itself to be felt. When you find it, sir, it becomes the very star you navigate your entire life by even when you forget to look up at it."

The butler stepped forward and interrupted them. "Ladies and Gentlemen, if you would please settle down. I believe the ladies are ready to commence."

Phillip swallowed hard at the lump in this throat. Mr. Carlton's eloquence was humbling but his heart clamored to agree that his love for Raven had become the star that he knew would effectively guide every step he took.

Lady Baybrook strolled out like a barge down the Thames and

began a rather over-pronounced interpretation of one of Cordelia's speeches from King Lear. "Alack,, 'tis he: why, he was met even now as mad as vext sea…"

Gratefully, Phillip acknowledged that his current blissful state numbed him to the worst of it. He stole a glance at Lord Trent and had to look away just as quickly to keep from laughing as the earl twitched and writhed like a man being pressed against a glowing hot grate.

Lady Baybrook finished with a braying crescendo and the audience applauded with the enthusiasm of prisoners tasting fresh air and freedom after years in a dungeon. Needless to say, it was clear the lady accepted it as an affirmation of her talents and not relief that she'd finished. She bowed and with a flourish of her gilt robe, sailed off behind the veil of the curtains.

After a few seconds, Lady Morley stepped out wearing a starkly simple gown of black with a swath of black silk covering her hair. The color flattered her full figure and something in the solemn way she moved, forced the room to an instant silence.

"Yet here is a spot."

He recognized the text instantly, surprised at the melancholy selection.

She went on in a sweet relentless singsong that conveyed only loss. "Out, damned spot! Out, I say!—one, two; why, then 'tis time to do it. Hell is murky! Fie, my lord, fie! A soldier and afeard? What need we fear who knows it, when none can call our power to account?—Yet who would have thought the old man to have so much blood in him?"

Tears poured down her cheeks, and no one doubted the madness of grief and torment that had seized this Scottish queen. "Here's the smell of the blood still, all the perfumes of Arabia will not sweeten this little hand. Oh, oh, oh!"

Her recitation continued, the strength of her performance never wavering even as the queen began to face her death. "To bed, to bed; there's knocking at the gate: come, come, come, come, give me your hand; what's done cannot be undone; to bed, to bed, to bed."

Several women in the room gasped, the men pressed fingers to their lips in rapt admiration and horror. Here, an unlikely actress had transported them from the room, and when she finished, they were lost. She stared out, and it was long seconds before they recovered their senses remembering themselves enough to clap. Then the applause took on a life of its own as the earl rose to his feet to evoke a standing ovation. Only Lord Morley kept his seat in a stubborn act of rebellion as if he alone could deny what he'd seen.

"Millicent the Magnificent!" the earl crowed. "Brava!"

"Brava, indeed!" Phillip echoed heartily.

Millicent's blush was very sweet and she wiped away her tears. Her expression of surprise only spurred on their appreciation. She bowed again and fled behind the curtain even as they continued to cheer.

Poor Mrs. Carlton came out as meekly as a mole into sunlight wearing a makeshift toga over her gown and Phillip's heart lurched to see her. *Hard enough to take the stage but after Lady Morley, it's quite a steep step.*

To her credit, with her hands shaking so hard he was convinced she was about to drop her painted torch, Mrs. Carlton didn't forget a single word of her speech. What she did forget was to raise her voice to reach more than a row or two but with her eyes locked onto her husband, she slowly fought her way through it, gaining a small bit of strength toward its finish. Phillip watched Mr. Carlton lean forward in his chair, enraptured from the first to the last.

"Bear with me; my heart is in the coffin there with Ceasar, and I must pause till it come back to me."

Mr. Carlton was on his feet as soon as she stopped, not even waiting for her to bow, moving so quickly to show his appreciation that he overturned his chair.

Everyone around him was charmed and all applauded, not only for the lady, but her husband's blind devotion to cheer for what was likely to be the quietest Marcus Antonius in the history of the Roman Empire.

"Brava!" Phillip joined in the accolades. "Bravely done, Mrs. Carlton!"

Mr. Carlton was a man bereft of speech, but he blew her a kiss and his bride colored, suddenly all smiles as she returned to her company behind the curtain.

Phillip shook his head and grinned at his seat mate. "A Complete Triumph, Mr. Carlton!"

"God, she was so—fantastic, I can scarce catch my breath!"

"You are a lucky man, sir," Phillip said.

"I know," Mr. Carlton sighed. "Ah, here is Miss Wells!" he redirected Phillip's attention to the curtains and it was Phillip's turn to fight for air. For Raven Wells was wearing a diaphanous empire gown evocative of a dream with a garland of ivy and roses atop her head. Gossamer wings of painted organza confirmed that she was not a creature of their world. Her black hair was loose to fall down her back and over her shoulders and Phillip realized with a surge of desire and admiration that even her bare toes peeping out from her gown conveyed a certain wildness and lack of shame.

A few in the crowd gasped at her daring but Phillip knew that every man in the room was under her spell. He smiled with a possessive pride that celebrated that he alone could claim her for his own.

"These are the forgeries of jealousy…"

Sweet and sure, she managed to be both timelessly wise as a Queen Titania would be but also eternally innocent. The speech was a sensual chiding to her beloved Oberon for his misbehavior and the consequences of the rift between them. She pleaded with her love for peace and Phillip's mouth fell open at the power of her pleas.

"No night is now with hymn or carol blest, therefore the moon, the governess of floods, pale in her anger, washes all the air….the spring, the summer, the childing autumn, angry winter, change their wonted liveries; and the mazed world, by their increase, now knows not which is which…"

She cast a spell on the room but Phillip was at the heart of it. Here was his fey fairy woman, wild and untamed! Raven was a creature in her element before them and he marveled at how fate had brought him a woman without comparison.

Then the curtains pull back and all the women have changed their costumes, either as fairies or apparently, Lady Morley, wearing a large paper-machier donkey's head as the cursed love of the Queen. Lady Baybrook was the wall between the lovers wearing a large grey cloak sewn with vines and small woodland creatures. Comedy reigned as it became the famous play within the play from Midsummer Night's Dream. The women all took multiple parts, with poor Lady Morley with her giant donkey ears dipping into the other actresses' faces demonstrating that her talents for broad humor matched her touch for tragedy. Her voice was muffled by the cage of paper and fur to make every nonsensical line more ridiculous. But it was only when the wall refused to hold her arms up any longer that the audience gave in to a roar of laughter.

Lady Baybrook put her hands on her hips. "A lady of quality is barrier enough to any romantic tangle!"

"Oh, cruel wall," Raven improvised. "Pray do not crumble until your cue!"

She was rewarded with more and more laughter as even Mrs. Carlton playfully added to the fun as her wig became turned around when she came too close to the cumbersome donkey. "Pray guide me to my spot, Queen Titania. I seem to be blind."

Comedy became farce and the earl rose to his feet. "Oh, god! Shakespeare is spinning in his grave and I do not care for I think I have laughed myself senseless! Enough, I beg you! Mercy, ladies! Let us all have you take a bow and then see to some toasts to our incomparable little thespians!"

The ladies awkwardly formed a line and curtsied or bowed as they could within the limits of wings and masks, accepting the praise of the audience as graciously as they could.

"Take that damn thing off, Millicent! You are making an ass of yourself!" Lord Morley barked.

His unfortunate choice of phrase made several guests laugh, and the lady in question shyly tried to slip back behind the curtains to comply with her husband's command.

Lord Morley's patience was at an end. He walked forward to grab the cloth ears only to have his wife clutch at the headdress in a strange tug-of-war. "Millicent! Take that damn thing off!"

"No!" a muffled cry rose up, and chaos began to take hold as the earl sought to restrain his friend and Raven and Mrs. Carlton held onto Lady Morley to prevent her from being pulled apart.

Everyone was on their feet, some frozen by the spectacle of a lord of the realm wrestling to pull a paper donkey's head off of his wife but others were pushing forward to offer assistance to one side or the other.

"Nooo!" It was an inconsolable sound but in one vicious move, Morley achieved his goal and he held the donkey's head aloft, like Perseus holding an equine version of Medusa's head for all to see.

"There!"

For a split second, there was raw silence at the shocking maneuver. Then Lord Morley was howling in fury. "Where! Is! My! Wife!"

A new chaos unfolded as it slowly registered that the woman he had unmasked who was now cowering on the floor was not the lady in question.

"Kitty?" the earl asked. "What is the meaning of this?"

Raven deliberately stepped in between the maid and Lord Morley. "We meant no harm! She took the part at my bidding!"

"Where is my wife?" Lord Morley barked again.

"You are making a scene where there is no cause for it, Morley," Geoffrey said calmly. "And you are ruining my evening."

Lord Morley's gaze narrowed. "Something is afoot. I can see it on her face."

"My face? Whatever do you mean?" Lady Baybrook asked. "What is the meaning of this display, sir?"

"Not you, you old cow!" Morley snarled. Silence descended as shock and horror warred for the room's attention. "Her!" Lord Morley extended a pointed finger directly at Raven. "What have you done, you little witch!"

Phillip had heard more than enough but Raven answered him before he could get past the bodies in his way.

"I?" she batted her eyes. "I cannot think of an accomplishment I can claim except proving you to be a fool after all."

Lord Morley's rage carried him forward, hands twisted into claws intended for Raven's throat. But Phillip tackled him without hesitation, driving him into the curtains that tore and covered them both. With the blanket encumbering them both, Phillip instinctively took advantage and kept a tight hold on Lord Morley to prevent him from lashing out.

By the time some of the men in the room had freed them both, Morley was practically foaming at the mouth in frustration. "She proves me a fool, does she?" Lord Morley tried to shake off the hands that held him in check. "Where is my wife? You'll tell me this instant or I'll kill you, Raven Wells!"

Several female spectators cried out in alarm at the threat and the earl signaled his butler. "Send for the authorities. It seems Lord Morley has abandoned his senses."

"Damn you to hell! There isn't a law in this land that keeps me from my wife!"

"Perhaps, but there may be something about threatening murder."

Mr. Carlton began to help Phillip to his feet but Lord Morley surprised all of them by wrenching free and kicking Phillip in the face. White hot pain sent him back against the floor, but Phillip gained his footing to prove that he wasn't defeated.

"Phillip! My love!" Raven rushed to his side and Phillip pulled her toward his back to protect her just in case Lord Morley made another charge.

"What was that?" the earl asked.

"Unhand me, you miscreants! My wife is—"

"Probably upstairs changing into her clothes and wondering what all this bellowing is about," Trent cut him off. "Walters. Send a maid up and fetch Lady Morley. In the meantime, hold his lordship fast." His eyes locked onto Phillip. "My *love?*"

"We should talk privately, your lordship. This is hardly the time or place to—"

Trent held up his hand to command silence. "I'll have it now."

The audience quieted again, the dramatic finale to the evening's performance far more than they'd bargained for. Phillip took in their curious gazes and then back to Raven. Her eyes were wide with hope and fear and he knew there was no avoiding it any longer. It was time for a grand gesture, though not as elegant a step as the one he'd planned for the morrow. "I wish to ask you for Raven's hand in marriage. For your blessing."

The earl's gaze narrowed dangerously. "I think not."

"Please! Lord Trent, I beg you to reconsider—" Raven cried out but another flurry of movement at the door interrupted the scene.

Mr. Walters strode up to Geoffrey to whisper something urgently in his ear.

The earl closed his eyes and then stepped forward to pull Raven roughly out from behind Phillip. Raven cried out at the bruising pinch of Geoffrey's hands and Phillip acted out of instinct, striking out at the earl to keep him from hurting her. It became a full on melee as his fist connected with Geoffrey's jaw. Raven screamed and Lord Morley began howling when Mr. Sheffield and several other men drove him to the floor when he moved to grab a fistful of Raven's hair. Chaos reigned again until all the combatants were separated. Lord Trent was breathing so hard in his rage, Phillip feared for him.

Hell, he feared for all of them.

CHAPTER 20

"*V*ery well, let's attend to one matter at a time, shall we?" The earl reached up to rub his jaw. "Lord Morley, your wife is indeed gone. Apparently the lady took the opportunity of tonight's theatrical to leave you, sir."

Shocked gasps rippled through the room. Lord Morley was finally allowed to stand, his coat lapel torn to flop about as if in echo of the donkey's ears. "Gone?"

"Gone, sir." Trent brushed off his own coat. "Mrs. Lindstrom is also missing and very efficiently with your wife's traveling clothes and personal effects so by all appearances, their run is well-planned."

"Have my carriage brought around immediately!" Lord Morley yelled at Mr. Walters, who signaled one of the footmen to carry the order out to the groomsmen. Lord Morley stormed from the room.

"My God!" Mrs. Carlton began to cry and put her head on her husband's shoulder.

Raven's hold on Phillip's arm was so tight, his fingers tingled but he had no desire to ask her to relax her grip.

The earl shook his head. "He'll have her back within the hour, no worries."

"No, your lordship. He will not," Raven said softly.

"Why won't he, little duchess?" Trent asked. "There has hardly been time for her to reach the village much less elude the chase."

"Because Lady Morley is inspired to stay ahead of him and fear can make a person very clever." Raven released Phillip's arm. "Lord Trent, I am very sorry for spoiling the play and for ruining the evening."

"What else is ruined, Raven?" Trent asked coldly. "You'll confess it now though I suspect I know the answer with Mr. Warrick flailing about on your behalf and that ridiculous endearment you blurted out."

"Your lordship?" Raven lifted her chin.

Phillip shook his head at the unspeakable dread that seized him. *Surely Trent doesn't mean to publicly humiliate her like this!* "No one and nothing is ruined, Trent! I want to marry her and I offer your ward the honorable protection of my name and my fortunes. There is no need for this!"

Trent ignored him. "Out with it, Raven. Have you disgraced yourself?"

"Yes." Her lips trembled but then she stood as proud as a goddess, despite her broken wing and wilting crown of flowers. "I am ruined."

Phillip turned her to face him, gently holding her upper arms as her eyes filled with tears. "No, Raven. To hell with him! There is nothing between us that I do not treasure and if we've been a bit... impetuous...then so be it."

"Impetuous?" Lord Trent scoffed. "You tumble my ward under my roof and speak of what? A callous rush to take what was not yours?"

His neighbors were openly lapping up every scandalous revelation and Phillip couldn't understand why Trent was allowing it.

"Raven," Trent sighed. "Look at me and tell me truthfully what you wish."

"I wish to spend the rest of my life with Phillip." Raven stepped away from Phillip to take her guardian's hands in hers. "I love him. Madly, completely and without fear. You have always taught me to be bold where others are cautious! Please, your lordship. Please give us your consent."

"I love her, Geoffrey." Phillip held his breath until the impossible finally happened.

Trent lowered his head and nodded slowly. "How can I stand in the way of true love? Even if it is so roughly born when I wasn't looking?"

Thank God!

"We never meant to trespass, Lord Trent. You have always been such a good friend to me." Phillip swallowed as his emotions warred inside his chest. "I swear that no man could love or cherish her more."

"Yes, yes," the earl said gruffly and pulled his hands from Raven's. "With so many witnesses, let's recover what we can. Decorum is injured past healing, but if you marry quickly, I will not stand in your way and will in fact, bless this union. If this is truly what you desire…"

Phillip squared his shoulders, unable to keep from smiling. "More than anything!"

"I want her honor restored with all speed, Warrick!" Lord Trent growled.

"You have my word." Phillip held his ground and put his hand out toward Trent.

Trent shook his hand. "Take my carriage. Gretna Green awaits." He signaled the butler. "Have their things packed immediately. Mr. Warrick and Miss Wells will be leaving us tonight."

Congratulations were sparse and many of Trent's neighbors began to retreat in haste, either to spread the delicious gossip they'd reaped from the evening or to distance themselves from the scandalous events.

Mrs. Carlton embraced Raven, still crying. "A bride deserves a better send off…"

Raven did her best not to give in to tears. "I could never ask for more than the happiness I feel, Mrs. Carlton. I have my hero."

Mr. Carlton shook Phillip's hand. "Best wishes to your future and to a long life together. May you be blessed, my boy."

Lady Baybrook shook her head slowly. "I for one am at a loss for words! Sensible women abandoning their husbands! Men brawling as if the earl's library was a tavern! And now I am to…smile and toss rice at this wretched distasteful proposal?" She made a dramatic sweep of her cloak, unaware that the family of squirrels sewn to her shoulders had started to come loose so that they now appeared to be hanging off her breasts. "My dignity cannot bear it."

She sailed out of the room and to everyone's great credit, no one laughed until the library door was firmly closed behind her.

"We will also take our leave, Lord Trent." Mr. Carlton gathered his wife back into his arms. "It is too much commotion for my wife, sir. We will leave tonight and send the carriage back for our things in the next few days. As you know, my estates are not far and frankly, I think the goal of ending our holiday on a memorable note has been achieved. I don't think my heart can take anymore surprises."

"Of course, of course!" Trent conceded. "God, what a mess!"

Phillip and Raven saw the Carlton's only as far as the library door and then rushed to oversee their own preparations.

Raven reached her room only to face a small flurry with Kitty sobbing and packing trunks as quickly as she could. Raven did what she could to help, seizing her prettiest clothes and fighting the battle between pure joy and anxious anticipation of leaving her guardian's care and everything that she'd known for over seven years.

"Kitty, you must stop weeping! I'm to be a bride! It's not as if you're sending me off to Newgate!"

"I know! Wishing you happy. I just…cannot see the house without you." Kitty pressed the heel of her hands against her eyes. "What will *I* do without you?"

"Besides marrying that handsome groomsman you've been mooning over for years and living happily ever after?" Raven teased. "I cannot imagine."

Kitty managed a weak smile. "You are a romantic at heart, aren't you?"

"Always." Raven surveyed her trunks then looked back to her maid. "Whatever I've left behind is yours, Kitty. Consider it a gift from your grateful and impossible mistress. A small repayment for your bravery tonight to help with Lady Morley."

"I was so scared when Morley started to pull off my mask!" Kitty shuddered. "I thought he would murder me then and there!"

A knock at the door interrupted the conversation. Kitty opened it to find Mr. Walters outside the door. "The carriage has been pulled around. His Lordship insists that there is no time to spare."

"Her trunks are ready, just here." Kitty stepped back to allow the footmen access.

Raven sighed and then squeaked in misery.

"What is it, Miss Wells? Have you changed your mind?" Kitty asked.

"No. It's just..." Raven held out her arms and turned slightly to model her bent paper fairy wing. "I forgot to change out of my costume. I'm—leaving as Queen Titania of all things!"

Kitty nodded and gave the men a fierce shove out the door with the trunks. "Out! All of you! Out while I see to my lady one last time! Tell the earl she'll be down before they've finished strapping those to the back of the carriage!"

PHILLIP WAITED ANXIOUSLY at the bottom of the grand staircase under the cold watchful eyes of Lord Trent. The carriage was waiting and the servants were finished putting in the trunks.

"Lord Trent. In all the shouting, there was one thing I meant to say."

"And what was that?" Trent asked.

"I meant to say that I am truly sorry. I should have found a way to speak to you sooner and I never wished to—cross you. I fell in love, sir. There was no malice in it."

Trent nodded and slowly crossed until they were practically face to face. "I don't believe in regrets."

Geoffrey pulled him into an embrace, an awkward tight thing that caught Phillip by surprise. Relief flooded through him, the gesture of forgiveness robbing him of speech. He embraced his future father-in-law and sent up a silent prayer that it was a good sign that they were past the worst of it.

"I am here!" Raven called out as she ran down the stairs. She was a vision in cobalt blue with a velvet cape to match and the men released their hold on each other instantly.

"Good. Let's see you out!" Trent nodded and the footmen opened the front doors. "It's a full moon so you can travel straight through without delays and be married tomorrow. Send word when the deed is done."

Raven hesitated before him, choked with emotion. "You have been so kind to—"

"Yes, yes, I am kind. No tears. I hate tears, Raven. Go. Just go. For goodness sake, you've insisted on your happiness and now you have it. Don't linger to make a useless scene now." Lord Trent kept his hands tightly clasped behind his back. "Godspeed, Raven Wells."

Phillip guided her out and the strange farewells were over and the carriage was already out of the oak lined lane leading to the manor before she could think to lean out the window and wave.

Phillip kissed her to soften the blow of their rough start and Raven cried in his arms for all that was lost but also in amazement for all they'd won.

Godspeed.

CHAPTER 21

*I*t was less than ideal to ride through the pitch black of night to Gretna Green and Phillip held her close in the rattling confines of the carriage for two hours before he decided that they'd gone far enough.

He signaled the driver to stop at the next decent inn.

"Are you sure, Phillip?" Raven asked.

He smiled. "We'll get there soon enough and since in this instance, we have no angry guardian to elude but instead are going happily of our own accord—I don't see why we can't stop and get a decent night's sleep."

Raven cheered instantly. "I would like to be fresh for our wedding and not a bruised and travel weary harridan."

He laughed. "Well, when you say it like that, we should have stopped in the village six miles ago!"

She rewarded him with a kiss to his cheek and a playful nip at his earlobe. "Be kind, husband-to-be!"

"I shall do my best to please you, wife-to-be."

The carriage stopped soon enough and the lovers alighted at a small humble establishment set at a crossroad. Raven waited at the carriage and helped point out which small valise to take inside while

Phillip went ahead of her and paid the innkeeper for the best room he had available.

As they wearily climbed the stairs, Phillip held her hand with one arm protectively out to keep her steady. The innkeeper pointed at the door at the end of the hall. "It's there. Here's a tray with some libations for you and your missus. If you need anything else, just call down the stairs."

Phillip awkwardly took the tray and Raven smiled as the man abandoned them to their own devices. "He was...very gracious."

Phillip laughed. "Nothing but the best for you, my love!"

"Come, let's see what your coin has bought us for the night." Raven pushed open the door and sighed happily. It was a simple room but clean and not as drafty as she'd feared. For several minutes, they quietly tended to the comforts of the room, lighting the candles and seeing to a fire, airing out the bedding and pouring the wine.

Raven loved the domestic magic of knowing that each gesture was a hint of what it would be in the years to come. She would learn the way he liked all things and strive to please him. *Or at least, make an effort when I can...for surely no wife has ever managed to make her husband smile at all of life's turns. I'll attempt it and earn this happiness that is threatening to make me cry.*

"Wine, my love?" Phillip held out a ceramic cup to her.

She wrinkled her nose. "I would rather not."

"I expected your refusal." He set the cup down. "But here, come sit with me and let me give you something long overdue."

"Is it a kiss?" she asked eagerly.

Phillip laughed. "Here. Look for yourself."

He waited until she was sitting next to him on the settee by the fire and then held out a small black leather box.

She took it shyly, opening it to reveal a ring of gold inlaid with pale blue topaz and diamonds. "Oh! It's lovely!"

"The stones reminded me of your eyes," he confessed. "I wanted to give it to you after I'd talked to the earl but...we didn't exactly make it until tomorrow as planned, did we?"

"Nothing went quite as I'd planned, Phillip."

He nodded. "I know. But I want you to see this as a sign, my darling, that all will be well. Even if you and I tend to back into our joy by accident and happenstance, it doesn't mean that we lack intention."

"A proper engagement ring," she whispered.

"Because we are about to be properly married, Miss Wells."

"Yes!" Raven's eyes shone with unshed tears and he placed the ring on her hand where it fit perfectly by design. "I cannot believe that it is possible to be this happy and still manage to breathe!"

"Perhaps we'll get used to it," he said and then leaned over to kiss her cheek. "I only wish we weren't the only ones to know this bliss." He sighed. "I hope poor Lady Morley finds some measure of safety."

"I am certain she has."

"How can you be? He left in his carriage and with two outriders only minutes after she was discovered missing. I think in this instance, your optimism has to accept the inevitable. He will have her in hand long before sunrise."

She smiled. "Hardly. I knew she couldn't outpace him on a muddy road. What a ridiculous proposition!"

"Then...how could she have eluded him?"

"You are assuming she left just after the play."

"Didn't she?"

Raven was glowing with her mischievous triumph. "No! I had her things loaded into the Carlton's carriage and Lady Morley and Mrs. Lindstrom were hiding inside the coach with the curtains drawn. It wasn't until the Carltons left that I knew they were properly away, and Lord Morley would never think to search that neighboring estate. Not in time," she added. "Mrs. Carlton's tears were quite convincing, were they not?"

"H-how? The Carltons were in on it? Truly?"

"Mrs. Carlton was. But she knew her husband well enough to know that the instant he was informed of the truth, he would happily become our accomplice. Lady Morley and her maid will hide at the squire's for a few days and then make their way to Belgium where Millicent has relatives."

"What truth?"

"Lord Morley was cruelly beating his wife and she feared for her life."

"My God! Why didn't you tell me?"

"I was sworn to keep her secret and she was terrified that your male loyalty to her husband or aversion to her illegal escape would betray our plans."

"I would never have done that!"

Raven reached up to smooth out the anger on his face. "Phillip. It wasn't my secret to give away and no reflection of my trust in you. It was Millicent's nightmare and I know you respect her courage for ending it."

He sighed. "Yes. But enough of that now. I cannot think of the worst. Not tonight." He stood and lifted her up into his arms to carry her cradled against his chest, striding toward the room's narrow bed.

Raven giggled as they landed on the surprisingly soft feather mattress. "I look forward to sleeping in your arms."

He laughed at the lack of room that ensured an intimate night. "It seems you'll have to."

Triumph made them both bold. They undressed each other in a slow dance, relishing the new balance between them. They had each toyed with their power over the other, conquering or surrendering in turn, but now it was as if they had nothing to prove. And it was the most heady and freeing sensation of all.

The candles were extinguished until it was firelight alone that cast the room in shifting shadows and warmed them.

"Surprise me, Raven. Rule me."

"As you wish."

His dare spurred her on as she pushed him back onto the bed. Then with one mischievous look at Phillip, she knew that he would deny her nothing. Raven knelt over him, thighs spread on either side of his head, her sex at the ready for his kisses. He gripped her hips and lifted her up to set his mouth against her. She was in control but it was Phillip's tongue that set the pace. She danced in a gypsy's gyrating turn atop him, touching her own breasts, lifting them for him, reveling in the wicked thrill of it.

Shifting up, she turned as an even naughtier idea came to her. With his tongue darting up inside of her and teasing her clit, she seized his cock in both of her hands and lowered her mouth over it, sucking and stroking him. Her imagination took hold as she imagined that he was already inside of her, that his beautiful flesh was sheathed and resheathed in the grip of her muscles.

She came and lost her rhythm, crying out as a spasm of ecstasy robbed her of grace. By the time she came back to her senses, she could only look at him apologetically, for there was no evidence that she'd achieved more than her own satisfaction.

But instead he rewarded her.

He sorted them out to cover her with his body, parting her thighs, delving into the throbbing flesh between her legs with his fingers and when she arched her back to come again, he plowed into her against the bedding, rocking his stone hard flesh up into the yielding channel of molten fire that fit him perfectly.

As if she'd been made for him, carved from ether and prayers by a benevolent power and Phillip drank it in. He made love to Raven until their strength was spent and they could give no more.

As the fire died in the hearth, they lay chest to chest and nose to nose, whispering of their hopes and dreams for the years to come. Phillip sighed and his last thought before sleep claimed him was of pure satisfaction.

Won. I won.

CHAPTER 22

Phillip watched Raven as she dozed on the seat across from him. Neither of them had slept much the night before and he reveled in how their passions ignited his soul. Instead of exhaustion, he was experiencing a sense of renewal and invincibility as if the world were his for the taking with Raven at his side.

What a force she was!

He liked the man he'd become in her company and entertained himself imagining the life they would share together, the children they would sire and the accomplishments of their years.

Rain began to fall softly and added another layer of sensation to their isolation inside the tiny world of the carriage's interior. Here was a universe with only Raven that made him happily forfeit the existence of any other.

Phillip carefully stretched out his legs so as not to disturb her or her voluminous skirts and tucked his hands into his pockets for warmth. The folded paper was an unexpected discovery, so he pulled it out with mild curiosity. The black wax seal bore the Earl of Trent's arms and Phillip turned it over in his hands.

Warrick - To be opened after your marriage.

Phillip smiled. He guessed that the earl had slipped the note into his pocket when they'd been making their farewells and that it was no doubt, some clarification of Raven's dowry or a formal wish for their marital happiness. After one glance at his lady love, Phillip impulsively decided that since they'd hardly waited to do anything in its proper order he didn't see that the earl's directive should be exempt.

He broke the seal and began reading Trent's familiar handwriting with a comfortable sigh.

And then there was no thought of comfort.

DEAR WARRICK,

By the time you read this, I expect you will have the rise and fall of the ocean beneath you as you and your precious bride sail forth. What a lovely notion!

There are just a few things I neglected to tell you before your departure to rushed nuptials. You have married a creature that can only be described as a piece of penniless garbage without legitimate name, fortune or reputation. Her dowry is a feral love of pleasure and a talent for ruin. Enjoy! I have it on good authority from my male servants and several houseguests that your new wife is sure to provide you a heated bed to rival any whore in London.

What a lucky man you are!

Raven is a brilliant player, don't you think? Be sure to convey my thanks to her again for assisting me in your downfall. What a dutiful ward she has proven to be!

Best of all: you claimed her out from under my roof with multiple reliable witnesses in attendance, announced your eternal love and then swept her away despite my "protests". What delicious fodder for the scandal mills! This match will provide entertainment for our peers for years to come. No worries. I'll dispatch the news to the papers so that not a salacious detail is ever forgotten.

Farewell and Good Luck.

I win.

Trent

THE WORLD HADN'T COME to an end because he could still hear the sounds of the horses, the rattle of the carriage wheels and the soft patter of the rain against the roof and windows. But he couldn't feel anything. Not the paper in his hands or the fingers that held the vile message. He couldn't feel his own heartbeat or the breath slipping past his lips.

Phillip had no idea how long he remained in that strange suspended state but when it ended, it ended with a roar of pain and rage that overtook reason. He hammered on the carriage wall to signal the driver and the horses pulled to a stop.

Raven immediately awoke at the commotion, startled by the sudden sound of his distress, her eyes confused as her dreams were wrested from their reach. "Is it...highwaymen? Are we—in danger?"

"Get out!" Phillip kicked the carriage door open. "You vicious little bitch! Get out of this carriage!"

"What?!" Raven sat up, ramrod straight, her face draining of color. "What have I done? Are you mad?"

He thrust the letter at her and began to physically bundle her from her seat. "Here. Take it and have your piece of the triumph, you heartless witch!"

"Phillip!" she screamed as she was propelled onto the road, her skirts instantly spoiled by the mud. "What is this cruelty?!"

"Sir?" the coachman asked in alarm.

"Throw her baggage off! Miss Wells will be leaving us here!"

The man ducked his head and immediately obeyed as the lady began to wail in horror. Her trunks and hatboxes made a pitiful sight as they were ejected without ceremony into a mound alongside the hedges.

"Phillip! Stop this madness, I beg you! What can have happened? You—I love you, Phillip! We—all that has passed between us—to what cause can—"

"Don't! Don't you dare speak to me of love! You whose very existence makes a mockery of that sentiment! What do you know of love?" he demanded, his voice shaking with emotion. "How dare you! What a fool I was to hand my heart over to a practiced whore!

Though to my credit, you are quite the actress, Raven. I believed in you so completely I never even slowed to ask how such happiness was possible. But I know the answer now, don't I, my darling!"

"I don't understand what you're saying! Please, Phillip. I dare to speak of love because it is the only language I know when I look at you!" Raven reached up to try to catch one of his hands but Phillip pulled away as if she were a leper.

"You think to play me for Trent? To laugh at my ruin? Well, you may get a chuckle or two from our adventures but I'll be damned if I ever lay eyes on you again! Good bye, Raven. Rot in Hell!" Phillip slammed the carriage door closed, drew the curtains shut and banged on the wall to propel the carriage forward.

He closed his eyes as her screams echoed down the lane until he couldn't hear her anymore and it was all he could do to keep his own screams of rage and pain from slipping past his lips.

Damn you, Raven Wells.

CHAPTER 23

She cried out for the carriage to stop, for the world to right itself, for her beloved Phillip to come back to his senses and to her arms. She screamed until her voice deserted her and raw braying sobs gave way to silent tears. The rain began to fall in earnest and Raven stumbled back to the strange remnants of her life. Leather trunks and pretty hatboxes were so out of place in the grass, perhaps as out of place as she imagined she appeared. The dark green silk of her dress was a streaked muddy disaster and she could do nothing but wait.

She'd been dreaming about a grand ball. It was a waltz and Phillip was there in a vaguely erotic embrace. The room was gold and Raven was laughing as her slippers barely touched the floor.

And then Phillip was shouting and—

Not wearing a bonnet.

A practical voice inside her head interrupted the plummet of her thoughts. Raven hiccupped in agony and blindly put the unread letter that Phillip had given her into her skirt pocket. *God, yes. Let's not think of him. Let's not... It's raining and I have a bare head. Bonnet. I have half a dozen.*

She knelt next to a hatbox and pulled out an impractical thing with peacock feathers and a wild flourish of organza on its crest, only to drop it onto the ground. *Useless thing that.* She tried another and another, only to add their exotic colors to the ruin of the scene around her. One of the bonnets was made from a fabric so fine it nearly melted at the touch of rain and she laughed mirthlessly. *What a useless thing! Like me, yes? Silk and feathers and...I'm crumbling at the first touch of cold and rain.*

The last box finally yielded a smart little straw bonnet with a frivolous lavender velvet bow that had once made her smile. She removed the bow to let it fall at her feet before putting on the bonnet that offered some slight protection from the elements.

The search for a coat or wrap came next and the casualties of that search were even more voluminous. By the time she'd located a reasonable cloak lined with fur, the ditch was strewn in a rainbow of gowns that fluttered pitifully in the wind as they fought against the rain that was driving them into the earth.

A small handled leather case for her jewels and any small item of immediate worldly value was the only thing she collected until she finally stepped back onto the road. Raven looked for a long time in the direction that Phillip's carriage had gone as if staring might yet summon him back.

Practiced whore.

Heartless bitch.

Rot in Hell.

It had been easy in the orphanage to dismiss insults because one heard them so often that they were expected. But from the startling source of a man who had sworn his eternal love, decried her every part as priceless, from the person that only hours ago had made her cry out his name in pleasure...

There's a cut that may never stop bleeding.

"Phillip." Her voice was rough and she winced at the croaking sound of it. Then nodded for it seemed only right that the last time she would speak his name would have no beauty in it. Here was a loss she wasn't ready to measure but Raven Wells was not a piece of delicate silk to lie down in the mud and gulp down shame.

She turned her back against the direction that Phillip had taken and pivoted to face the other way.

It was human nature to want to look back, to take one last view of the life she had had, the love she had lost and the dream that had died in the violence of minutes. Raven nodded in acceptance of the longing to linger and then lifted her chin one firm inch in defiance.

Raven Wells tightened her grip on her bag and began the long walk through the storm.

And vowed to *never* look back.

FINIS

EXCERPT FROM BOOK TWO:
LADY RISES

rologue
Kent, 1866

PHILLIP STUMBLED up the stone steps of Oakwell Manor, his legs numb from the pace of his ride. His clothing was sodden and his coat felt like it was woven from iced iron as it swung against him. He pounded on the door, caught in the furious storm of his emotions.

Walters opened the door with an expression of mild surprise but was no match for Phillip's momentum. He was past the man before he'd spoken a single word, marching toward the beckoning light in the ground floor study.

"Trent!" he roared before he'd crossed the threshold. "Trent! You son of a bitch!"

The Earl leaned back in his chair and calmly set down his book. "Warrick!" he said cheerfully. "Not on your honeymoon?"

"You bastard! You well know that I am not!" Phillip ran a hand through his wet hair to pull it off his face. "You know more than anyone!"

"Yes, that is probably true." Trent was all smiles. "Did you come by for enlightenment?"

For one fleeting breath, Phillip nearly launched at the smug figure seated before the fire, his hands curling into claws prepared to tear the earl's throat out—but god, more than the satisfaction of murder, he desperately wanted to understand why his life had taken such a horrifying turn. "Yes. Enlighten me, old friend."

"I once promised to be your mentor, did I not? But I failed you, dear boy. You crossed me long ago and I neglected to punish you. Let's just say, that I vowed to set things right."

"I...crossed you? How?" Phillip's breath caught in his throat. "Long ago? That courtesan? Are you—is it even possible?"

"I assure you, it is more than possible. It is a certainty. You had the audacity to mount another man's prized mare without so much as a by your leave, Warrick." Trent's cheery demeanor began to fall away. "You made a mockery of me! But you've got the bitter end of it now."

"That was years ago! You—said you'd forgiven all!"

"A bit of a lie, that. I apologize."

"So all of it? Raven was—all of this was some kind of scheme to destroy me in payment for tupping a slut you once bought a few dresses for?"

"I had her keeping!" Geoffrey screamed and then went as still as stone. "No need to revisit that now. But how is your bride?"

"What do you mean how is my bride? I've come here to fetch her! Tell her to come down, Trent!"

Geoffrey's mouth fell open, his eyes alight with excitement, as he left his chair at last. "Tell me. Tell me what happened when you read my letter, Phillip. Tell me every detail and I will do what I can."

Phillip could taste ashes in his mouth at the sick and strange turns in their conversation. But he wanted Raven. "What is there to tell? I read the letter while we were still in the carriage en route to Gretna Green."

"Impatient boy! Did I not write on the envelope that you were to wait until after your marriage?"

"That? *That* is your complaint now?" Phillip had to clench his jaw and count to three before he could continue. "Raven was asleep and I found the note in my pocket. I didn't think it would make any difference... But it made all the difference, didn't it?"

"You didn't make your wedding vows?"

Phillip pressed a hand to his eyes, the grip of a headache starting to clamp down. "We weren't in any hurry. We'd stopped along the way and...I never thought to rush."

"The letter."

"Yes! I read it! I was bored and it was pouring rain to make for slow going and I read the damned thing!" Phillip dropped his hand, fury carrying him past the pain. "It was an ugly scene, sir! I woke her and threw her from the carriage! I ordered the driver to ride on and had every intention of never turning back!"

"Brilliant!"

"Was it? The carriage barely made it to the next hamlet before the mud became too much and the roads impassable. I was drinking at a roadside inn and cursing both of you to the fiery pits of Hell when it —occurred to me that I'd made a mistake."

"Only one?" Trent prodded with a laugh.

"Raven is mine. The lack of dowry stings but money can be made, sir. If there is one lesson you did convey before descending into madness, it was that one. As for the rest of her villainy, I..." Phillip swallowed hard. Here was the harder hurdle. His instincts said that Raven was an innocent when he'd taken her that first time, and he'd have sworn her maidenly barrier was not contrived with theatrics. But the vile flatness of the language the earl had used; the vague threat that every male servant inside this hall was even now laughing at him behind his back because they'd had her in every room of Oakwell Manor... Phillip started to choke on the bile that rose up his throat. "It is between us. I will attend to her failings and if I have to keep her under lock and key, then so be it. Tell her to come down."

"And my promise to notify the papers?"

"By all means," Phillip countered. "Of course, you'll have to include that she was *your* ward and under your supervision. The implications will be that you approved. Approved of every misstep and may have even encouraged it. I fail to see how your reputation is not also forfeit, so by all means. Contact the reporters. I'm sure they will have all manner of questions about how to raise a vile slut as one would a house cat."

Trent nodded. "Good point. Oh, well. I will savor my victory in private then." Geoffrey brushed off his hands. "Thank you for stopping by. I'm sorry I can't offer you a room but you have so much to do, sir."

"Yes. Keep your petty revenge, you piece of shit. Now, Raven. Tell her to come down," Phillip repeated, a new chilling fear snaking up his spine. "The weather delayed my return but when she wasn't... She'd abandoned all her things but I know she would have found her way back home."

Geoffrey tugged on the bell pull. "She is not here."

"She has to be here."

The earl smiled. "No. Don't be a simpleton. A woman abandoned in a rainstorm by the side of the road with dark fast approaching? Use your imagination, boy. Go on. What do you suppose can have happened to your Raven by now?"

"God. No." In his glorious upset, he'd seized only on the one outcome. She'd thrown a fit by the side of the road, dumped out her trunks in a temper and then marched homeward until securing transportation of her own so that she could return to the welcoming arms of her nefarious guardian and his praise for her conquest.

But now...his imagination achieved a dozen horrifying scenarios in the space of a single heartbeat and Phillip staggered back as if the earl had struck him in his midsection with an andiron.

Trent clapped his hands in malicious glee. "Look on the bright side, baron. Your whore has given you a gift and freed you of worry. Death is a quick solution and she's either drowned in a fen, succumbed to the cold of exposure or actively hung herself from the first obliging tree she could find." The earl shook his head. "It amazes me how women are so resourceful!"

"I murdered her," Phillip whispered.

Strong hands began to seize his arms and Phillip's misery was compounded by the humiliation of realizing he was about to be forced from the earl's house.

"Nonsense! And what do you care?" Geoffrey scoffed and then started to laugh. "Although it is an unexpected thrill to see you so devastated, Warrick. For that, I shall never be able to repay you as you've made years of planning and all my pains worth it."

No matter what wicked part she'd played in his downfall, the guilt he felt at her destruction was paralyzing. "All this? Because years ago, I fancied myself in love with Lacey?"

"Was that her name?" the earl asked.

Phillip's gaze narrowed, his rage returning in full force, choking him. Only the footmen's hold kept him from hurling himself at Trent.

"I'd forgotten," Lord Trent admitted softly. "Throw him out and see that he is never admitted to my property again. Good bye, Warrick."

"This isn't the end!" Phillip struggled as the footmen began to haul him backward. "I'll make you pay!"

"Stupid to threaten a man of rank and with witnesses, sir. You'll do no such thing. Or I'll start asking what happened to my sweet little ward and you'll swing from a hangman's noose." Trent's brow furrowed with impatience. "It's ended so prettily, don't spoil my evening, boy! Out!"

They had him through the foyer and pushed down the steps with the added indignity of a beating to ensure that it was all he could do to crawl back onto his horse. The heavens reopened with an icy downpour and before Phillip reached the gate, his stallion was lame.

He dismounted and limped toward the village.

Broken.

A man broken with nothing.

Phillip Warrick was lost.

ACKNOWLEDGMENTS

Forget the rules. Let's do this as if no one is looking because let's face it. Few people bother to do more than scan the acknowledgments so I say that means I can run a little wild here. Before I thank anyone else I want to thank the readers that have not only waited patiently for this next incarnation of Renee Bernard to take place—but they never stopped believing that it would be worth it. Man, I hope I don't let anyone down! Because those emails and FB posts and amazing notes you've sent…it's humbling. I owe you my sanity. I hung on because you let me know that you wanted me to keep going. So, thank you. If anyone gets acknowledged, it's you.

I want to thank Deborah Elissagaray for being an inspiring and beautiful person who not only makes AMAZING wines (Ursa Vineyards… I kid you not, people…) but for being that friend who never fails to reflect the best in this world. Deborah, you were an oasis for me and books would not have happened if you weren't so generous with your time and your support. When the bullies came and knocked me down, you poured me a glass of wine and let me believe I could conquer the world.

I want to thank Anne Elizabeth for defining generosity of spirit and for always keeping things level. My circle will grow and change as I go, but you will always be at my side and that's something I don't think an acknowledgment can really cover. Sheila English is in the same boat. If I tried to include all the reasons for being grateful to have you in my life, it would just turn into another book...

Lindsey Ross, when I said I wanted to write a trilogy about a sexy, dark villainess and break every rule I knew about romances, you actually sounded excited about the idea. So, bottom line, when no one else was up for the game, you raised your hand and I remember thinking that if nothing else, I would write Raven's story for you. Thank you for being there and for putting up with the craziness.

I have to thank Nancy Goodman for being fantastic in every way that a friend and fellow author can be fantastic. Where have you been all my life? I also have to quickly thank Danelle Harmon for making me rethink snow, the meaning of life and my need for a dog. Danelle, you are stuck with me now.

And I want to thank my awesome Street Team, Bernard's Bombshells, for rocking it! I love each and every one of you! I mean it. When we make it big, we're going to have our own mini-retreat and I'm going to spoil you rotten!

And last but never, never least, I have to thank my Mom. Even though I know it's practically a given that moms think their kids are the best, it still amazes and humbles me when you say those things. Showing you off at RT in New Orleans was one of the highlights of my life and no matter where this roller coaster takes us, I will never forget the magic of sharing those days and giggling over eating way too many beignets. (Is there such a thing as too many beignets? Seriously.)

Made in the USA
Las Vegas, NV
28 December 2023